499

Lightning Field

a novel

DANA SPIOTTA

SCRIBNER

NEW YORK LONDON TORONTO SYDNEY SINGAPORE

SCRIBNER
1230 Avenue of the Americas
New York, NY 10020

SCRIBNER and design are trademarks of Macmillan Library Reference
USA, Inc., used under license by Simon & Schuster,
the publisher of this work.

For information regarding special discounts for bulk purchases, please
contact Simon & Schuster Special Sales at 1-800-456-6798 or
business@simonandschuster.com

Designed by Kyoko Watanabe
Set in Electra

Manufactured in the United States of America

1 3 5 7 9 10 8 6 4 2

Library of Congress Cataloging-in-Publication Data
Spiotta, Dana, 1966–
Lightning field : a novel / Dana Spiotta.
p. cm.
1. Los Angeles (Calif.)—Fiction. I. Title.

PS3619.P65 L54 2001
813'.6—dc21   2001020306

ISBN 0-743-2-1261-4

Lightning
Field

Her hands are white and long and lithe. They make elusive, fleeting frames—flirtations of shapes, really—on anything they touch. Anything in the world. I would follow those hands out to the desert. I would. I would watch them on the black leather curve of the steering wheel. I would watch them light a cigarette with the glowing car lighter after it made a low pop and smelled vaguely of burnt food. And I would watch them as she gestured when she spoke, as if she were weighing air or beckoning someone near. At times I notice her watching her own hands, admiring their white elegant angles and delicately draped bones. When I notice her watching her own hands, I look away, my eyes shy from shame.

"Mina," she says, and I like it when she says my name and leaves it there hanging, like a statement, or barks it, "Mina," like an order.

"Leave everything," she says. "The one thing you can't leave behind is the thing you absolutely must."

OK, OK, sure, but we take money. Lots and lots of it. Lorene's more than mine. And her car. But nothing else. Not a book or a change of clothes. Not a ring or a stocking or a journal or a fountain pen.

We lunch at a truck stop. Laminated menus with heart-healthy options. Pale coffee and everything smells like syrup.

"Look, sugar cubes," Lorene says, dropping one after the other into her coffee, letting each one balance on the spoon, then submerging it until it becomes saturated with the pale brown liquid.

"It reminds me of a commercial," I say.

"Yeah," Lorene says, "me too. Why do I keep doing this," she submerges the cube slowly and watches it absorb coffee, "why do I get such a kick out of this."

"I don't remember which, maybe not sugar," I say. "Maybe the cube is used as a demonstration."

"You mean an absorbency demonstration?" Lorene asks.

"Yes, exactly something almost like that. Absorbency."

"There were so many demonstration commercials. So visual, so scientific."

"Sugar cubes. I really like sugar cubes. Why'd they go and get rid of sugar cubes?" I say, all of a sudden extremely sad about it.

"Packets, perhaps, offer labels, small type, nutritional information, a higher ability to sanitize. Last longer. There's the anticipatory shaking gesture, loading the granules into one end of the envelope so it can be torn without spilling. Improved delivery system of loose granules versus cubes. Dissolves easier. Makes it easier to use more. Nefarious plot to destroy my body's ecosystem. Yeast- and microbe-feeding, inner-organ-caramelizing sugar," Lorene continues, stirring her coffee, pushing it back and taking another drag on her cigarette. "But it makes the coffee palatable, which in turn makes the cigarette enjoyable, which in fact makes the morning bearable."

The waitress is adjusting her stockings. She thinks no one is looking, and she pulls at the fabric of her skirt, nearly jumps with the pull. She reaches to the back of her knee, gets a handful of nylon, inches it up, a minor hike, then tries again, through the skirt, the little jump-hike.

"A perfect system. Airtight. No complaints," I say.

Still, I know that isn't it. No good reason to get rid of cubes. An object of unremarked-upon delight rendered less than what it was. It's what Michael would say, it's the sort of pleasing detail you never seem to notice until one day it's gone.

Lorene slips two fingers through the handle of her coffee cup and braces it against the fingertips of her other hand. She lifts the cup to her mouth, closes her eyes, and sips the hot, sugary liquid.

But maybe, just maybe, that's not it either. Maybe sugar cubes seem pleasing just because they're gone, and that kind of detail brings you pleasure only as a contemplated lost thing, the pleasing nature of it is realized only because of its absence.

One Month Before Leaving: The Cocktail Hour

Mina watched him, examining his profile at twenty paces. Mina watched him, half-shadowed, through a window, half-lit with the amazing dusk light, even, or especially, L.A. movie-fake dusk light that could be thrown by a switch in a sound-stage. A fading soft pink light that made her long for soundtrack swells, the softness making her think she longed for every person she ever thought she should have loved a little more, but really it was only a scented-hanky kind of nostalgia, an antiques shop nostalgia, or, finally, a cable channel documentary-type nostalgia for people and places you never even knew, not a longing for home, but a longing for "home." Mina had a weakness for this kind of bungalow dusk melodrama. When the whole city caught her off guard she found an emotional attachment to its past and she read its ugliness as its charm. It was then she felt she had finally got it, that it was her place, fleetingly, if only because of the light and its fading glow.

He was part of that light, and she could not stop watching him in it. Through their window. From a distance. Not just that, but his unawareness of her watching.

For the past two hours she had done the unthinkable, the violate: she walked. First through the Vista Del Mar neighborhood of old tiny 1920s bungalows, sort of Spanish Colonial with odd Moorish and Eastern flourishes, stuccoed and surrounded by palm trees, so arranged and moderne they seemed carved in Bakelite. Car-free, in summer ballet flats, the only one besides gardeners and children, Mina walked along curbs and looked through interior-lit windows, the fading dusk light affording anonymity, the TVs and stereos and nearly audible conversations providing a schizoid soundtrack—strange juxtapositions of familiar radio sounds with other people's lives at an audio glance. Sometimes just a name, spoken and unanswered, hung in the air, or whole arguments at high volume. She could pause and listen for hours to fragments of conversations about dinner or car keys or mail.

She had walked the long way from Max's apartment in the Hills, then headed down Gower past Sunset and Santa Monica. The streets had already thickened with homebound cars, five o'clock sliding into six o'clock, a special segue time that was once called, by someone, somewhere, the cocktail hour.

People used to slip seamlessly from Hollywood General on Highland, from all the rattan and wickered bungalows on the Paramount lot over on Gower, to, where? Maybe the Cinegrill at the Roosevelt Hotel. To a padded banquette at the Dresden, around crescent-shaped tables seemingly designed for fourth-wall-theater staging, or an *In a Lonely Place* lonely stool at the bar at the Brown Derby, or Musso and Frank's. Or a dozen other bars, long gone, that used to line Gower and Hollywood. Gower's Gulch. Actors, extras—cowboys and gladiators. And all those suit-spectacled execs, in her mind all as young and three-buttoned and black-and-white as the photo of Irving Thalberg her father used to have in his study. It had that name, Gower's Gulch, back when it had a history, used to be called Gower's Gulch when cowboy-actor extras hung out, waiting in between calls at Paramount and Hollywood General. Mina's father told her (and where did he learn it, because it was well before his time, this ancient Hollywood history he seemed to know a priori and with detailed authority) they'd still be in costume, bursting into bars as if they were Wild West saloons, Max Factor'd pink plastic cowboys getting drunk, starting fights, feeling the difference between real bottles and breakaway glass. Mina walked past the corner minimall with its Western-style burnt-wood hanging sign. *Gower's Gulch Convenience Center.* Nice touch, and she wished, particularly when she passed the huge wrought-iron and adobe gates of the studio, that one teensy cowboy-actor bar had been salvaged, a secret perfect dive where she could have a drink that would afford her sanctuary, someplace simple and unself-conscious, a modest, sad dilapidated spot, an "establishment" offering mere refreshment and a minute of quiet solitary enjoyment—a real drink, away from the ubiquitous new and bright and sandblasted. A bar, her father would have said, where there is no shame in ordering a scotch. Where a person could smoke a cigarette unmolested. But there were none, and Mina instead wandered into the old Paramount studio store, where in a montage of lightning edits—color, hand, pocket, money, color, exit—she quickly bought an armful of expensive cosmetics. A teal eye powder. A tiny brush to apply it. A waxy-smelling lipstick in a blue red (Caput Mortuum) made for black-and-white photography. Translucent face powder, loose, of course, and the fluffy real-horsehair brush to apply it. A bottle of Red nail polish. A concealer stick, in Bisque #9, Medium Fair. She left quickly, buzzing with the secrets of the universe in her paper bag, followed by, within seconds, dire regret. She opened the bag, there on the sidewalk, out in the sunlight, and stared at the Red nail polish, all wrong, really, the polish—actually a Midwestern near-red, sort of weathered-barn colored—not what she wanted at all. She stood there, dismayed by her failure to even address the shelf of red nail polishes—the Original Real Red polish, so close to Raven Red and Scarlet Red but darker, oddly, than Carmine Crimson Red—how she avoided the issue altogether, just grabbing Red, not even Simple Red, and of course the polish would never be exchanged, but tossed in a drawer with thirty other nearly perfect unused colors, until it became old and its chemical components started to separate, all the colors finally turning into an umber-orangey rusty red topped with a pool of murky colorless oil. She would just have to wait until she could devote the time, until she felt up to determining which, finally, would be Rita Hayworth Red. She barely resisted the urge to toss the whole bag of cosmetic purchases and go back in, to do it right, microexamine the red polishes, head back in there and trial-and-error the whole row.

Spend hours on it. But instead she ambled in a zigzag on the pavement, staggering vaguely away from the place, her head looking back while her body went forward, nearly stumbling into a young woman approaching her, unexpected and unnoticed, seemingly curb-sprung, touching her arm (touching her!) on the sidewalk.

"Excuse me, ma'am, may I have a second of your time?"

Mina felt the inexplicable but undeniable horror of an unseen stranger putting a hand on her bare skin, her forearm. She jerked her hand body-ward. At a sideways street-wary glance the woman seemed a beige sort of person, not brunette but simply brown haired, her whole body exuding a monochromatic nylon Nude- or Flesh-colored drugstore stocking shade (bagging and bunching at the bone-apparent knees and ankles). Her imprecise, maybe-young body was all forward leaning, both slender and awkward at once. The girl nevertheless held herself with a rigid, remarkable poise that must have required exuberant discipline. Her brownesque look was clean and groomed—it wasn't fashionable, but it at least required effort to produce, at least conveyed some self-attention. Mina continued walking—she didn't like being called ma'am. She didn't like looking at this girl, either.

"Please, ma'am, just one second," she said, and Mina again felt the girl's hand touch her arm. It made her jump, this aggressive yet barely there cool hand touch. Mina's body already transformed by adrenaline, she turned hard on the girl, fit to bark or even yell. It came that easily—her urban-accessed rage, huge reservoirs of hostility at the ready, induced by a touch or a wrongly chosen noun.

"What?" Mina said, and the sound of her own voice animated her. She felt the word shape itself in her mouth, the way her body almost shook on the stop of the *t*. She knew she would repeat the word, that she would enjoy hurling it at the girl, the huff of breath moving the *w* over the *h*. Only in a certain volume and intensity could you hear and feel the near hiss of the middle *h*. "What?" she said again, and the girl did not recoil or back off, but instead met her look and returned it.

"You feel anger. You feel fear. You jump when you are touched." The girl's eye contact did not waver. Mina made an audible inhale, looked away, and an audible exhale. These days, on the unwalked streets of this place, mere attention and description, mere articulated detail of attention passed for brilliant perception and near extrasensory abilities. People so unused to being addressed by strangers that simple exposition was wisdom. She sighed her boredom, shook her head, but exaggerated it.

"You have heard of St. John Solutions?" the girl asked, pamphlet-proffering, now losing the eye contact. The glinting, glossy pamphlets—vitamins, holistic therapies, meditation, massage therapy, aromatherapy, past-life therapy, empowerment workshops, colonic irrigation, self-actualization, life counseling. At St. John Spirit Gyms. Mina had of course seen them everywhere. Little sandblasted glass-fronted places, in plastic-colored blue and that franchise drywall white. Even Lorene now went to St. John Ataractic Asepsis Therapy twice a week. At her hairstylist's suggestion. Her hair and skin texture apparently indicated pathologies. Deep cosmetic pathologies which, evidently, were never merely cosmetic, but cosmological, in fact. Mina shook her head and started to walk away. The girl continued speaking.

"What you most want to run from is where you should go. Ask yourself the following questions: Do you feel anxiety about the decisions you have made in your life? Do you have diffi-culty sleeping? Do you have occasional vulvic itching? Do you feel fatigued? Has your skin lost its resiliency? Do you suffer from inability to concentrate? Do you crave sugar? Do you sometimes wonder if it's all worth it any longer?"

Mina, for the first time in ages, wished for a car, a rolling up of windows, a radio to blast.

"Do you feel a longing for home? Do you suffer from yeast overgrowth, chlamydia, urinary tract infections? Do you feel you're entitled to more? Do any of the following describe you—"

She walked quickly and heard the girl's voice gradually fade.

"—lonely. Full of rage. Hypervigilant. Bipolar. Bruise easily. Sensitive to household products. Addicted to television . . . alco-hol . . . the Internet . . . prescription drugs . . . junk food . . . illicit drugs . . . shopping . . . OTC drugs . . . sex . . . plastic surgery . . . herbal dietary aids . . . psychotherapy . . . sleep . . . cigarettes . . . working out . . . caffeine . . . Visine . . . foods con-taining MSG . . . self-improvement therapies . . . foods con-taining aspartame . . . twelve-step programs . . . foods containing Olestra . . . thrill-seeking of any kind?"

Of course, the car radio was where this St. John guy lived (or flourished, an opportunistic fungus or virus sprouting great flora of new growth, the oxygen-deprived, exhaust-basted brain cells of all those traffic-ensnared captives waiting to be contam-inated). But—Mina had to consider—maybe they had some-thing. Maybe *she* had something. Candidiasis. Opportunistic microorganisms. Undistinguished vaginitis. Couldn't her ill-nesses at least be distinguished? She felt a longing for cures. It was part of the siege of local optimism. A belief that nothing is irrevocable, nothing couldn't be solved, answered, and quickly, too. It was the schizophrenics, or schizoforensics, of this utopia/dystopia place—things deeply, pathologically wrong, but instantly and infinitely remediable. She enjoyed this kind of self-obsessed hysteria as much as the next gal, but the aesthetics of it, the strip-mall franchises, the slogans, the girl's panty hose—how could Lorene, *Lorene,* even consider? Then there was the unfortunate thing about confidence men who truly believed what they said. The unbearable sadness of it not being true.

Mina was behind now, she would barely have time to get ready for work, she'd have to call Lorene from home and tell her she'd be late, again. She hurried along the long stretch past Hollywood Memorial Cemetery. Ask, go ahead (no one did)— Cecil B. De Mille and Jayne Mansfield were buried there, sure, but everybody knew that. But she knew Tyrone Power, Norma Talmadge, and Marion Davies. Clifton Webb (she used to know them all), Dabney Day, and Virginia Rappe. Famous dead people and people famous for being dead. It had amused and pleased Jack that she remembered these names. The more obscure, the more her father laughed. She knew, eventually, them all: Westwood Memorial (Marilyn, sure, but also Donna Reed, Natalie Wood, and Dorothy Stratten), Forest Lawn Hollywood Hills (Stan Laurel, Ernie Kovacs, George Raft, and Freddie Prinze), and Forest Lawn Glendale (Spencer Tracy, Jean Harlow, Alan Ladd, and Tom Mix). Mina still could recall all of the names, though none of that mattered now.

Ordinary.

She liked, on these strolls from Max's, to dream up the most painful, most dread-inspiring phrase and try it out on her psyche.

Her father would never forgive her for being ordinary.

Pretty good. Something she might tell a therapist. If she had one. But no one had one anymore. People had prescriptions, which were much less time-consuming. Precisely because no one bothered with it, therapy appealed to Mina. Therapy. It had an old-fashioned, retro charm to it. She fantasized about it, her perfect audience of one, her pad-scribbling, attentive psychotherapist. Eyes full of dewy sympathy. The sympathetic nods. Brow-furrowed and lip-pursed listening to Mina's self-theories. The best phrases were just south of being true. And when she thought them, she felt she was shaking out blankets and pulling back curtains or stepping onto a scale. When she spoke them aloud, she became convinced they were dead-on, red-hot, epiphanic, life-changing revelations. Which was the problem, really. Assertions, of course, take on their own lives.

She would never forgive her father for being ordinary.

Pretty good. This is also what she knew about the confidence men. She could be one, too.

Mina passed the south edge of the expanded cemetery near Fountain. The cemetery was getting bigger all the time. In the future of Los Angeles, it would be just the fake adobe stores and the cemeteries. It was nearly seven. She had to finish this tour now.

Mina used to tell strangers about her father's death.

The extraordinary death of an extraordinary man, Jack Delano. The pills, barbiturates, and the drink, Jack Daniel's. The rope—a vintage sound cord, double knotted. Sometimes it was a shotgun in front of the photo of a smirking twenty-five-year-old Orson Welles. Wistfully she would add, what became of that photo—she wished someone, one of them, still had it. Nastier, the terry-cloth robe tossed aside, the final Pacific swim.

People always believed what ridiculous stories she told of his death. Mina could drive these fears into sentences and then move onward, a veneer of calm. There were, in the weave the present made with the remembered past, telltale signs, warnings and intimations to be read, evident to the merest self-contemplation. And in the fleeting seconds before Mina's hand actually hit her forehead to rid herself, actually jar herself, of too intense a contemplation of regret and reproach, fissures of other possibilities engulfed her, the landscape of her alternative, other life glimpsed. She thought of a parallel universe, similar but smarter, mocking her in this one.

Perhaps because she worked in a restaurant, or maybe because of her own food obsessions, when the dinner hour came around, and she glimpsed kitchens through windows and heard loose segments of family dialogue, at once strange and familiar, she found she couldn't resist thought runs of them all. She first thought of him. Her brother. And Jack, her father. And even everyday David, husband of three years, through the pink dusk-lit window.

She imagined her brother eating something institutional and monotextured, perhaps laced with his resisted psychotropics, or at least an undertaste of hospital. Michael was in Alcatraz gray and grainy black-and-white, eating in mechanical gulps—although she'd never actually seen him eat that way, she couldn't help imagining it now. And for symmetry's sake, she tried to imagine a quick cut to Jack, the repressed fat barely kept at bay with diligent counting of caloric values, everything he ate meticulously low-fat and macrobiotic. Bragged about sourdough bread from two-hundred-year-old starter, perhaps Indian-touched in some way. Her husband, David, was of course strictly cardboard and plastic, the food already congealing on arrival. There was something so sad to her about eating alone, and something particularly unbearable about men eating alone. Maybe because only women actually preferred to eat alone, while such solitude made men vulnerable. Then Mina stopped, just shook her head slightly. It had become easier than she would have thought, this not thinking. Lately, her afternoons at Max's fixed that for her.

In another lightning edit —

Max's jean-clad thigh pressed between her legs. Or just him saying yes in the lowest of voices in her ear. Just thinking about it made her press her thighs together as she walked, made her careless and even smile to herself. Something there, in his gaze as she moved on the bed. The way she felt it even with her eyes closed. Being watched. She could close her eyes now and feel it, an intoxicating glow of attention not so far off from how the world looked with her eyes closed, warm darkness somehow shot through with sunlight, somehow seeing by feeling, probability shot through with suspense and memory and a tiny bit of faith, even.

Past the cemetery, Gower lost its interest, and Mina could have moved more quickly, could have felt urgency, should have, but she refused.

The afternoon's tiny gestures, the taste of his fingertips, the seconds when they finished their drinks and his breathing changed, and she walked accordingly, meanderingly, kicking at gravel and feeling the edges of her shoes drag on the seams of the sidewalks. She looked at her feet as she walked — see the girl kick at the pavement. See her swing her arms.

When Mina had finally walked up the stone path to her house, she stopped at the point where she could look into David's office. His computer was on, as it almost always seemed to be. She stood there, as she had last night and the night before. It seemed she always ended up needing a bit more time, and the odd waiting and looking had become habit, even inevitable. She could spend her life in segues, commercial breaks, cigarette pauses, walks from, hallways to. She felt most herself hesitating before doorways and listening to the dial tone on her phone as she mustered the energy to call, or to hang up. These sideways, solitary moments when she could catch the world from the margins or at a glance. At the seams of things, or the awkward lulls the editor would leave out. She was convinced the truth of things could be glimpsed in these off-sides and in-between places. It was just these sorts of telling nonmoments that are most noticeably lacking in affairs. The incidentals that happen to couples when they move from one ordinary thing to the next, revealing the intimate ways people negotiate the world—pouring cereal, or addressing a letter, or the shape their mouth takes when they are on the phone with Mom. And any attempts to introduce them with Max seemed unbearably intrusive, a breach, a kind of rudeness. What's worse, she'd begun longing for them. An almost insatiable curiosity and desire for boring quotidian details of Max's life. She'd become even reluctant to leave him afterward, the horrible telltale thing—wanting to linger. She wanted to elongate her late afternoons at Max's, stay in bed until they felt nearly stuck together, until they spoke and revealed odd things to each other, stick around until a meal was suggested, or a back rub, or a bath—anything but separating and that lump of afternoon light that hit her when he closed the door behind her. Today she had stayed in the lull, couldn't help it, but in fact—and she knew this—the lingering and elongating tended to make things only sadder and weirder.

He complained of an arm falling asleep. Not complained, but said, "Honey, can I just shift my arm, can we just . . . yeah, much better," but it was not just repositioning, it was incremental separating. First it was the arm out from under her, then he had to go to the bathroom. Then she heard him pee. Next the move to the shower, and it was his not-so-subtle signal that the cuddle, bed part of their afternoon was over. And if Mina defiantly stayed in bed throughout the shower, as she had today, if she remained warm and quiet until he came out in a towel, he would act as though it did not bother him, in fact he would appear pathologically unbothered, severely without bother, and this would bother her and she would tell him to come here, as though she was longing to touch him, but it was really a battle of wills at this point, a war of trite longings.

"Would you like a cup of coffee?" he asked. "Another cigarette? An apple? I just have to check my voice mail. It will only take a second."

Was this a sort of kindness? But it wasn't really the marginal, in-between, down-time realness that she missed, was it? The real thing—the thing she could not bear, the thing that betrayed the hidden quotes around words like *love* and *passion*—was his intensity undone, his ordinary glances, his loss of interest in looking at her. The steady slackening of desire, the dreadful slide to a quiet indifference. And his videotaping, which occurred with increasing frequency, somehow seeming to ridicule her need for his attention, to caricature it, but she still couldn't resist. It felt as if they were documenting their waning desire—precisely the opposite of the attention she really wanted. But it was a kind of attention, still. He was in a way right—there was no reason to stick around. She didn't love him, she wasn't really feeling affectionate. She just wanted—

for as long as she could feel want—to put her mouth on his body every time she saw him, and she wanted him to see it in her face and let it hover in the space between them, making the air electric and the world myopic, making every ambiguity and doubt kaleidoscope to convey this desire, at this moment, in this place.

Mina continued to watch David through their window. He put his tea down, and his fingers moved on the keyboard again. She found this oddly erotic, his unknowing, her watching. She couldn't bring herself to go in, she wanted to continue watching. The way he never looked up, her husband, David. She waited in this interim space. Things seemed momentarily alien, they hinted at other readings, other interpretations.

Maybe her father used to watch her mother like this, when he left his girlfriend's apartment. Maybe he would watch her make dinner through the window, unable to move.

Probably not.

Lorene Baker's house was not difficult to clean. Lisa found that even at a leisurely pace she would be finished well within the allotted time period. On Thursdays, at Mike Birnbaum's apartment, she had to work quickly to get it all done in four hours. She had to be organized, had to have a schedule and a discipline about it. First put the sheets in the washing machine. While those washed (thirty-five-minute cycle) she put the tile and porcelain cleanser in the toilet bowl to soak. She sprayed the tub with Soft Scrub Tile, Grout & Tub Cleaner. She rinsed the crusted blue gel Colgate Platinum toothpaste from the water glass, the faucet, and the toothbrush holder. She rinsed the sink sparkling, scrubbed the soaked toilet bowl with a round brush until it flushed clean. She sponged the hair and dust from the screws where the toilet seat attached to the toilet bowl. She wiped the base and the sides of the toilet, where a coating of dirt and dust and micro skin flakes unfailingly accumulated. Next she sprayed the shower curtain with Anti-Mildew Fast-Acting Formula 409 and sponged. If this was let go for even one week, white clumps of bacterial residue started to accumulate in crevices and folds. Then the shower walls, scrubbing the grout between the tiles with a small brush. Cleaning was finally all maintenance, a dutiful prayer against decay, and only finally winnable, manageable, if practiced unfailingly and diligently. Last, she mopped the bathroom floor. Lisa changed the wet sheets to the dryer (forty minutes) and put Mike Birnbaum's dirty clothes into the washer. Socks hard—no, crusty—with his week-old sweat. His undershorts. She was doctorally immune to all of it. Now the whole process started over in the kitchen, beginning with the dirty dishes, which he always left. With rigor and precision (and not a little satisfaction) she finished the kitchen in time to remove the sheets and put the clothes in the dryer, iron the sheets and put them on the bed (air-smelling, warm) by the time the clothes were dry and could be folded and put away. Lisa was expert at this, she snapped order into Birnbaum's life and disappeared. An invisible force.

Lorene's place was different. Lorene sent her very apparently valuable sheets to an out-of-state laundry that specialized in cleaning sheets properly. All Lisa had to do was unfold the undyed brown paper from the packages and put the sheets on the bed. Her bathroom and kitchen were not in much need of scrubbing. She appeared to use neither. Lisa went through the systematic washing and scrubbing, anyway. She was a gesture, a luxury, for Lorene, or maybe a backup system. As she dusted Lorene's living room (book-lined, many plants) she would play

Lorene's records. Actual vinyl, with a needle in a groove, with static noise around the music. It made the music more tactile, less airless, somehow. Lisa swore she could hear it better than when she listened to compact discs. She enjoyed the strange old torch songs or big band stuff Lorene inevitably had on her turntable. Stupid songs about lovers and boats that made you feel like you were your grandmother — or in a movie about your grandmother. Music made for daydreaming.

Sometimes this music made Lisa emotional. She thought of Alex and Alisa. And at first this was nice, but somehow, some way, she would get it into her head that they were sick. Something in a look or feel of morning dressing, she would remember as toxic and symptomatic. Children do get sick, and mothers must notice these things early. And then Lisa would not be able to stop imagining her children ill. She imagined swollen lymphs and leukemias (just the word, the *kemo* part, so toxic and decayed sounding). Some horrible juvenile invasion of *E. coli* — what had she fed them, what some food terrorist might have contaminated. It happened all the time. Apple juice, organic spinach, for Pete's sake, an American mass-produced hamburger in a clean paper package — and what? Kidney failure, irreversible brain damage, coma, death. It starts with "I have a tummyache, Mommy." A sweaty forehead. Lisa would get faint and feel a hard round knot in her stomach. She would turn off the record player and hurry, heart racing, through the rest of her perfunctory duties at Lorene's. She would pray to herself, feverish, hysterical bargains and third-world-mother ancient incantations, until she could get herself to Mrs. Brenshaw and see her two baby loves.

She inevitably found them watching TV, jammy-faced and sticky. Hi, Mommy.

*   *   *

"Lorene, you feel very tense," he said. "You must try to relax."

"I'll never get there," she said. "It will take hours."

"Shh, just feel my touch," he said, blanket-voiced and comfort-toned.

"I am trying, damn it," she said. "Oh, there, yes, that spot. God."

"Stop talking. Shh." He pressed the spot relentlessly, a pressured, steady rubbing.

"You're very good. Very patient," she said.

"C'mon, give in, it's OK."

Lorene felt herself letting go, a slow, deepening undoneness that started with his mechanical repetition and radiated out through her body and finally to the clamor in her head. Her mouth became slack, she felt her tongue as a muscle, her eyes rested shut. She saw red, shot through with veins of light. He moved to the next spot and pressed deeper. An hour and a half of Tactile Hue Therapy. One hundred and seventy-five dollars at St. John Spirit Gyms, and well worth it, she guessed. Her St. John's counselor (actually, they were called "Healing Partners"), Beryl (not his real name and also the name of a quartz-looking heliodor yellow transparent crystal he wore around his neck, the pyramidal tip pointing to his heart), recommended touch therapy twice a week. Part of her prescribed Spiritual Exfoliation and Detoxification. She needed to be touched by another person. And she had to hire someone to do it, which was almost funny.

Red. She was supposed to think about the red she was seeing as he touched the parts of her he was touching. No, not think about, of course, but meditate on the red she was seeing. But that's not it either—she must just feel the red, become the red. That was the first color. Then Beryl instructed her to take control of that vivid, anxiety-tense red and make it into a peaceful medium blue. A low, saturated pacific blue. Then transform blue to white, make it drain slowly to a perfect celestial white of complete mind-body-soul equilibrium. But she had first to think of red. But not think, feel red, feel it turn to another color from someplace unwilled and natural in her person. She must "feel" the color and "see" the touches. All these "supposed to"s and "must"s in order to relax—it was nearly funny, wasn't it.

He switched to long pulling strokes on the back of her thigh. She felt where her muscles attached to her bones. It felt to her that he was gently lifting muscle from the bone, creating a space deep inside where everything was generally muddled tightly together, as if he shared the weight of her body for a moment. Lorene found this pleasurable, his going against the constant, everyday burdens of being a body. What did he feel, or see, or think, the toucher? The professional toucher?

When she was without money, before she had the restaurants, she had only her beauty, her taste, and her style to recommend her. She had to market professional glamour. Lorene guessed she must have been the first life-stylist. She figured out how to sell her life-style consultancy to the rich, particularly rich men. Men who spent all their energy making money and couldn't be bothered with how to spend it. Her first client was Joseph Walker, some sort of software tycoon. She was already a personal shopper then, starting at Neiman Marcus and then quickly going freelance, working not only to wardrobe Beverly Hills second wives in the taste- and wealth-indicating appropriate designers befitting their newly acquired positions, but she also helped men like Joseph do their Christmas, birthday, and anniversary shopping. She would buy perfume and lingerie for his ex-wife or his current girlfriend or his secretary. She began also to help him pick his own wardrobe, and even guided him as to what kind of aftershave he should wear, where he should get his hair cut, and what sorts of plastic surgery he might consider. In short, he paid her to tell him how to spend the money he worked so hard to earn. And Lorene found she could do this very well. When she had finished her makeover, and he looked, if not great, then at least vastly improved, he asked her to have a drink at his Westwood condominium. Lorene was, of course, a bit wary of Joseph having fallen into an infatuation with her (such transference was only natural, as dependency and desire get conflated in any quasitherapeutic situation, and some men—she particularly had suspicions about Joseph— just really got off on being told what to do), but she nevertheless met him to celebrate their success. She entered through the front door, and although Joseph was dressed well and impeccably groomed, she saw that her work in fact had just begun.

He poured Chivas Regal into thick-based hexagonal highball glasses.

"A man of your position shouldn't use glasses like these," she said, twenty-two and somehow supremely confident in all the things people found so difficult to navigate. "And only a very young man should pour blended scotch, or a woman. It's too cliché for someone of your age. You should pour some obscure but delicious Skye or Islay peaty single malt—Talisker, perhaps, or Ardbeg."

Joseph looked at her and smiled. He took out a ballpoint pen and indicated to her she should write it down. Lorene took the pen and then gestured with it.

"Get a Pelikan, or—just not a Mont Blanc, OK, Joseph?"

"What else, Lorene?"

"Well, where do we start? It isn't a matter of simply spending money. . . ." The art on the walls—there wasn't any. She would give him the names of some galleries. His music collection—awful. She composed a list. A certain amount of fifties and early sixties jazz, some well-chosen classical. And opera, lots and lots of it. She must offset his techno geekiness with something Old World and unexpected. Emotional and passionate. She found it easy. She just thought of what would impress and surprise her. What things she could discover in a man like Joseph that would intrigue her as a woman and make him seem unusual and impressive. It was a kind of love, or a creative sympathy. She put the pen down and pushed it toward him. He stared at her with a child's conspiratorial joy.

"Joe—which is a great name, by the way, no need to change that—Joe, you need one sort of eccentric thing which you must be quite passionate about. For example—German cabaret music. It's a little kinky, but in a classy sort of old-school way. Deep, throaty lesbian chanteuses, lots of Kurt Weill and women named Ute. What do you think?" He was nodding, smiling with her. She warmed to it. A real makeover.

Lorene, over a mere two weeks, had him paying attention to things he hadn't before—the sort of crucial details that indicated an examined life-style. She had him buy Egyptian cotton sheets of a ridiculously sumptuous thread count (they must be changed every day without fail). She had him collect wine—a cliché, true, but a necessary and sensuous amenity. A temperature-controlled, five-hundred-bottle cellar to start, which she filled with auction-bought bottles of Burgundy. ("You are either a Burgundy man or a Bordeaux man—you must choose and then be quite fixed in your opinion. You'll take Burgundy, it's much more complicated, and indicates sophistication. Not just mind-blowing Romanée-Conti, mind you, but you'll buy obscure monopole Grands Crus that only collectors and, of course, you know. And, yes, they are obscenely expensive.") He happily complied. She created a book collection—an extensive inventory of contemporary fiction, plus some obligatory modernist giants. She suggested he read the first chapter of each, when he could. He of course wouldn't, so she composed a paragraph or two about each writer and what was thought of him or her. She gave him a list of movies to rent. She, in short, created a life for him to come home to and slip into. He loved it. He had so little time. He offered her a weekly stipend, and she began to read the L.A. *Times* and the *New York Times* for him. She gave him weekly clippings of must-read items, which were further distilled to underlined, must-read sentences, to save even more time. She devised suggested conversation topics. When he had no time to read those, she offered short opinionated summaries of topics. She would even dine with him and give him conversation-style evaluations, a sort of dating report card, and give him (recited) precise notes. He was remarkably improved. Lorene imagined he could fool almost any woman into thinking he was interesting and had a full, exuberant life. From Joseph she had other men. Mock dates were very popular; she became quite succinct in her critiques: listen more, talk about this movie, hate that book. Make eye contact. Don't inflect your sentences so. Mostly she gave them lots of encouragement, and she discovered the sort of heart-wrenching, desperate loneliness of certain kinds of men. It wasn't that Lorene devised false lives for these men, as she sometimes accused herself, but that she had discovered she had a laser accuracy for reading other people's desires and vanities, and she could help them actualize those desires as styles and traits and purchasable objects in the world. She brought out the dark longings and turned them into lists and packages and simple, easy steps. Lorene learned what every confidence woman learns: all our desires are the same, we all want the same things, we are all desperate in the same way. And the first to declare an answer, especially a vehement, confident answer, wins. It was all in how you framed it. It was an issue of syntax. If you say, This is the one crucial detail that you must know, they will listen. And that was what she was selling, not a list of books—because, really, it was all so arbitrary—but a confidence, a way of thinking about the power of things to transform your life that made it work. She was selling faith, of course.

After a while it became difficult. Perhaps she had gotten too good at it, or thought on it a bit too much. Somehow, the relativity and arbitrariness of her own passions increased as she consulted for so many others. Everything grew quotes around it, and she found she started to give clients more perverse and obscure style advice. As her judgments became more divorced from actual feeling, she found herself increasingly mannered and overwrought. Her own fascination had pushed to a level of circular antitaste. She soon regarded her established passions as tacky and boring. She full-circled in such a singular pursuit of style that she started to forge strange ironies within her own already ironic pursuit of taste. She no longer recalled the chains of reference. She genuinely admired formerly despised things—the fat oakiness of a California Chardonnay, for instance, seemed witty to her. She loved, suddenly and deeply, the slyness of bombastic, terrifyingly dated seventies prog rock. She thought John Grisham novels would be so unexpected and unusual. She assured her charges that Paul McCartney was the coolest Beatle—his solo stuff, even better. She made them buy five-year-old hip-hop records. No more Kiehl's men's products, instead she recommended Dial soap, Aramis cologne. Finally, she found that her own taste was indistinguishable from her clients'. It had become hopeless; the men began seeming perfect as they were, so delightfully unstyled, chicly unconsulted, and she wanted to make lists of their books and records. She was desperate to hear what movies they saw and admired. She couldn't help them at all anymore, and she had ceased to enjoy any of it—a record or a book or a steak. She had to quit consulting, end her career as a life-stylist, Lorene having finally become so stark and minimalist, so desperate for simplicity and purity, that if she continued she'd need a stylist herself, someone to fill in her own blanks with confidence, focus, and consistency.

"Is that better?" Beryl asked.

Lorene had stopped, taken time to recover—spent a year infatuated with undyed rice-paper screens, felt a sort of ecstatic thrill throwing things in the garbage, listened only to Pakistani Qawwali chants, and cut her hair way too short.

Lorene sighed.

And now it had come to this, hadn't it? Lorene needed to hire someone named Beryl to touch her. She was more Joseph than Joseph now. It was worse than hiring someone to buy your art. It was paying someone to help you be yourself. Somehow, your confidence disappears. You need to loosen the tightness in your head, to make silent the colors in your body, to feel the low beating of your heart that seemed so alien and distant. Somehow find your way to some—what?

She had totally failed to meditate past red. Again.

She had an appointment with her contractors at Vanity and Vexation. She had to hurry.

He didn't die in a mangled car wreck. He wasn't stabbed or drowned in some sex-drenched confusion. No pills or rope or last pleas for help. He hadn't even really "disappeared."

He lived in a yurt in Ojai.

Mina held the phone in her hand, ready to call Lorene. There was a high-pitched tone and a message saying the cellular customer she was calling was not available or had traveled outside the coverage area. She listened to the message twice.

Since their divorce, Mina's mother always referred to him as "your father." How is your father? Tell your father I saw one of his films, or, Your father didn't like it when I cut your hair short. Never "Jack." She has never heard her mother say his name. She would even say to her current boyfriend, When I was living with Mina's father. . . . Aside from her refusal to say his name, her resentment never surfaced. It was as if she were speaking of a small child or an elderly person. Perhaps because of her mother's habit, it never occurred to her until recently that he was not merely her father, but her mother's ex-husband. Despite what Mina had learned, years after the fact from her brother, her mother never betrayed any low esteem for him. She was graceful in her privacy, or maybe it didn't matter anymore since he wasn't in the running in a real way. Or maybe (as her brother claimed) she merely forgave him. Mina, evidently, had not.

Mina suddenly and with no apparent hostility or self-awareness stopped calling him "Dad." He was "Jack." Even to his face, Jack.

Jack had amassed colossal debt. As much as he once had, it was double (triple) that he now didn't have. The debt loomed, tumefied and metastasized. Negative money is a powerful force. It grows unseen, becomes an ever-reproducing intestinal parasite, unfelt, or a self-replicating retrovirus, autoimmune, insinuating itself into the DNA of things, growing with you as it destroys you, and, most important, it would never stop.

Jack lived (perversely unaffected, Mina felt) in his yurt in Ojai—a placid, modest existence in the mountains with his new female companion, Melissa. When Mina last visited, she couldn't take her eyes off Melissa's large, braless, and preternaturally perky breasts. Melissa was all long legs and lips and tits. The silicone must have been from an earlier, more material phase of her life, because now she was feather-draped and yoga-poised, crystal-crusted and spiritually sanguine.

Mina rose before dawn, creeping out of the yurt while they slept. She was alone and anxious. The Santa Ana—surely it was one of those—was blowing from the northeast. It was a dulling predawn gale. Mina waited for them to get up, had a hazy glimpse of Michael waking in a room somewhere unfamiliar, and then she heard strange moans from within the yurt.

Mina realized, with enormous relief, their moans were controlled and in unison, of some meditative nature, not caused by exertions Mina would have found wholly inappropriate in the vicinity of the visiting daughter.

Jack and Melissa paid close attention to their breathing.

The dawn was upon them, the wind dying down as the sun rose.

Mina found herself helping Melissa sweep the yurt out in the early morning mountain light, a batted-eyelash, mottled dawn light, flirting through tree branches and from behind leaves and stone ledges, until the whole world had a gold-flecked glow. Mina wondered if Melissa always smoked pot first thing in the morning. Melissa did a classic, familiar mid-inhale gesture of drug sharing. How, Mina wondered, do we learn these exact gestures? How did drug culture develop protocol, actual cliché?

"No thanks, I'll stick to nicotine." Mina sat outside the yurt shamelessly smoking. "Outside the yurt, endlessly, shamelessly smoking," she said aloud. She loved saying "the yurt"; she inserted it into every sentence she could during her visit. "I'm going in the yurt for a lie-down." "Is there a feng shui direction I should sleep in the yurt?" "Is this a nonsmoking yurt?" "Do you have yurt-owner's insurance?" Jack and Melissa took these questions with surprising good cheer. They did everything with pacific, smiling faces. Melissa sometimes tried to talk to Mina. She sat next to Mina, crossed her long legs, and smiled one of those million-dollar California-girl smiles. Who could blame Jack?

"Where did you grow up, Melissa?" Mina asked.

"Boise, Idaho," she said. "You thought maybe Hermosa Beach?" And she winked at Mina, her crystal earrings glimmering in the dawn light. She had undeniably a new-age sort of guileless charm. Melissa was looking for the moon in the morning sky. She felt her menstrual cycles were connected to the cycles of the moon. Melissa, certainly, was connected to the moon in important ways. But no way more profoundly than menstrually. She discussed her cycle at length. "Your cycle," she explained, "can tell you things." She examined it, like entrails, for wisdom.

"The flow is really strong this month."

"Really? Smooth or clotty?"

"Stringy, stranded."

"Pain or no pain?"

"Aches, good aches."

"Cravings? Mood swings? Emotional disintegration?"

"No, not with the beetwort tea, the dong quoi, the hemp oil, the sage-burnt incense, and the daily affirmations. Just rapturous orgasms at the drop of a hat."

Thanks for that detail, girlfriend of Jack.

"Mina, have you ever heard of St. John Solutions?"

"No." Mina smiled.

"I took 'Understanding Menstruation, the Advanced Seminar' there."

"It changed your life."

"You'd be surprised."

VIDEO #1

TITLE: FIRST TIME

AUDIO IN:

MAX (OFF SCREEN)

It's not on.

FADE IN:

Extreme close-up of a GIRL on a bed, youngish, long hair, looking slightly off camera.

MAX (O.S.)

It's not on.

                    MINA
Is that why the red light is on?

                   MAX (O.S.)
Grainy, black-and-white, cinéma vérité girl.
Open your pretty mouth and talk to me.

                    MINA
Is this a sort of foreplay?

                   MAX (O.S.)
It's a video of a girl on a bed. It's the girl. It's the
girl being filmed by someone who finds her
interesting.

                    MINA
I don't think it's interesting. I don't think I like it
much.

The GIRL has her head down. Her long hair blocks her face.
She has her legs crossed and her arms crossed over her legs.
She stares at her toes. The camera moves closer. It moves to a
close-up of her bowed head and long hair.

                   MAX (O.S.)
Close-up on girl. Handheld, wobble-fisted. Is it
home movies? Is it art? She's shy, she doesn't
look up. She doesn't speak. We move in close to
her long blond hair. But it's such pretty hair. I
wish it were in brightest Technicolor. I think
you should be in brightest yellow, reddest red.

Rainbow-painted fifties American Technicolor.
You could dazzle us with your long blond hair.

GIRL pushes her hair behind her ears, looks at the camera.
Her face is pleasant, symmetrical, round. Her eyes are large
and her mouth is serious. She shakes her head.

> ### MAX (O.S.)
> Lovely. The face in view. The eyes, the lips.
> Those full girl-next-door lips. Reddest red. Can
> they speak?

> ### MINA
> This is not amusing me. This annoys me.

GIRL looks away. The camera pulls back, to show her on the
bed, body folded into itself.

> ### MAX (O.S.)
> Tell me why you're annoyed. No, tell me
> something else. Something I don't know. Tell
> me about when your uncle came into your
> room at night and made you promise never to
> tell. Tell me about when you and your college
> roommate got drunk and kissed each other's
> breasts among CliffsNotes and fingernail polish
> and you both swore never to mention it. Tell me
> about when you first cheated on your husband
> and wrote a confessional note, which you tore
> up, swearing to yourself it never really
> happened. Tell, tell, tell.

> MINA
>
> Nothing like that to tell.

> MAX (O.S., FIRMLY)
>
> Then make it up.

> MINA
>
> No.

> MAX (O.S.)
>
> Tell me about the fantasy you have of being tied up by a stranger. He blindfolds you and makes love to you while your parents are in the next room. Or your husband. Or the man you saw on the street that you imagined unzipping and feeling against a wall as his hands undid the buttons on your dress. Tell me.

GIRL starts to laugh, shaking her head. She takes her handbag from the side of the bed and pulls out a pack of cigarettes. She puts one in her mouth, tosses her head back a bit and strikes a match, lights it, inhales. She blows smoke in the camera's direction.

> MINA
>
> It's to be one of those movies, is it?

She smirks a bit, shaking her head.

> MAX (O.S.)
>
> To light a cigarette while you're being filmed.

It's poetry, it's the American gesture. It's what
Jean-Paul Belmondo died for in *Breathless,*
his exhale on camera, his hopeless European
envy. The fulfillment of a thousand film noir
fantasies, blowing out smoke on camera. It's the
true American dream.

MINA

I don't smoke. I don't have secrets to reveal. I
don't have sexual fantasies to reveal. I'm an
unsuitable subject for this game.

GIRL takes another drag on her cigarette. The camera is static
on her.

MINA

I think I'll just bore you into turning the thing
off. Not out of resistance, but a genuine
inability to do or say anything worth filming.

There is a pause. She looks at the camera. She is waiting. The
camera is static. A minute elapses.

MINA

It's a waste of film. Or video, or whatever it is.

Another minute elapses. GIRL looks down, purses lips,
indicates annoyance.

MAX (O.S.)

You could leave. You could get up and leave.

                    MINA
What did the other women do?

                    MAX (O.S.)
What makes you think there have been other
women?

                    MINA
What did the other women do?

                    MAX (O.S. LAUGHING)
They usually take off their clothes. They do. Put
a camera on a woman, and sooner or later, she
starts to take off her clothes.

                    MINA
Liar.

                    MAX (O.S.)
Nine out of ten.

                    MINA
What did the tenth one do?

                    MAX (O.S.)
I don't know. You're the tenth.

GIRL starts to laugh. There is another pause. A real-time dead
space.

>   **MINA**
> Say something. Ask me something. Anything.

There is silence. Just video drone. The sound of breath. She keeps looking at the camera. She stops smiling.

>   **MINA**
> What else? What else happens? Do you ever
> turn it off, or does the tape run out?

Silence.

>   **MINA**
> How long does it take for the tape to run out? Max.

Silence. Mechanical whirring.

>   **MINA**
> How long?

Silence. Static, unmoving on her. She looks weary. A minute passes, she sits on the bed, examines her toes. She looks off camera, stares hard to her left at something unseen. She doesn't move.

>   **MINA**
> I can't stand this. It's not funny. I'm going to
> leave.

GIRL looks up at the camera. She looks at her toes. She looks back up. She looks directly into the camera, unsmiling. She moves her hands to her dress. She closes her eyes. She starts to unbutton. She opens her eyes. Fade to black.

TITLE: END

"Is this Mrs. Delano?"

"Who is this?"

"Is this Mrs. Delano?"

"Who wants to know?"

"This is Bill. I'm an old friend of your husband, Jack Delano. I've been trying to reach him."

"You're lying. And I'm not his wife."

"Oh, I thought—"

"You're not a friend. You work for a collection agency."

"It's crucial I speak with your father."

"I'm late for work."

"It's crucial I speak with your father."

"My father lives in Landgrove, Vermont. His name is Mitchell Howe. He is the high school football coach."

"You are not related to Jack Delano?"

"Do you mean biologically? Or legally? Or spiritually? I have no aesthetic relation to the man."

"Do you know how to reach him?"

"I have no knowledge of his whereabouts. He disappeared, didn't you hear? It's a great mystery. I have not seen nor heard from him in five years."

"If you hear from him, can you tell him to call Bill at 1-800-627-1818, extension 24, reference number *p* as in Peter, dash 4590?"

"You're an old friend?"

"Yes."

Mina stood holding the phone. She listened to the dial tone. She was late, but it was difficult to get going.

Mina's mother left Jack long before he "disappeared." She, her mother, rubber-banded all her credit cards together, placed them on the dresser, and left.

Mina had last seen her father on her one and only visit to Ojai. She had left Jack standing outside the Krotona Library in the Ojai village. Krotona was the name of a Southern California fin de siècle utopia. Jack told her the Krotonians read auras, didn't wear clothing, and spoke only Esperanto. Mina said good-bye to him, he hugged her, and as they pulled apart he winked at her, a gesture so long lost and utterly familiar it held her dumb and shaken. She felt a hot rush of childhood affection, a kind of swell that closed in her throat. She stared at him beneath the Krotona sign, tan in his strange sandals, and she had to turn away fast, hot tight tears and walking, walking. Fast. She walked past the Krishnamurti Library. She sobbed now in hate of this place, she hated this place, hated being here. Mina walked so fast she didn't notice the sun-haloed fire poppies, the buckwheat in swatches, or the gray-green thickets of shrubby oaks. She waited for her bus, unaware of the nearby citrus trees edged by low stone walls, not thinking of each stone fitted and balanced against the others by some person, slowly, some long, long time ago.

The drone of the dial tone was replaced by a wincingly high-pitched whistle and a voice urging her to hang up. This was followed by the usual staccato high-volume beeps, designed to make even the most dreamy of girls pull the receiver away from her ear and return the phone to its cradle.

Pleasure Model Enterprises

Lorene paced, narrating her feelings to herself. "I am feeling anger. I am angry," she said. This didn't help. She practiced her breathing at the bar. She tried to focus on her diaphragm, her inhalations and exhalations. Mina was hours late. Officially, one hour and twenty minutes late. Lorene had said seven, be here at seven to go over the bar construction plans, and to allow Lorene to make it to an eight-thirty Pilates class, followed by a massage and reflexology session at the St. John Spirit Gym, conveniently located four blocks from her nearly completed restaurant, Vanity and Vexation. Lorene breathed and consumed gulp after gulp of distilled water. She kept rubber bands around her water bottle. She started with ten. Her bottle held eight ounces. Each time she drained it and refilled it, she removed a rubber band. This ensured she would consume at least eighty ounces of water throughout the day, the minimum for optimal hydration, flushing of toxins, and clear urinary and colon function. She should consume up to one hundred ounces, allowing an extra eight ounces per ten cigarettes she smoked in a day. The extra water plus supplementation of vitamin C (one thousand milligrams every six hours, time-released, since C was water-soluble and not fat-soluble and would be expelled in her body fluids if not used) ensured some protection against the ravages of nicotine on her system, if not mitigating in any way the carcinogenic effects, which was certainly a losing battle, but not unsolvable, she was convinced, not impossible, but in any case a whole other supplement story, the cancer-fighting vitamins, herbs, and minerals contained in St. John Laboratories If You

Must Smoke for women, fifty-milligram tablets, $29.50 a bottle to Spirit Gym members. Mina's extreme inconsiderateness had increased Lorene's biostress to such a point that her system would probably render all supplements useless, anyway. The whole day a wash. And no exercise meant Lorene wouldn't be able to eat anything tonight except for a small piece of skinless organic chicken that she would swallow in approximately four and one half minutes, and a balsamic-vinegar-drenched wild green salad that she wouldn't finish at all. Lorene lit a cigarette and did what she wasn't supposed to do, which was phone Mina's house. David answered and she hung up, and tapped a new cigarette on the zinc-inlaid service bar from where she surveyed the progress of the workers.

At eight-fifteen, when Mina walked into the newly installed sixteen-foot trefoil-shaped oak double doors to Vanity and Vexation, transported from the remains of Lorene's previous establishment, the highly successful Dead Animals and Single Malts, it was apparent Mina's tardiness was not going to come up, Lorene merely nodding at her and then looking hard at her nearly finished bar/club room, mid-distance staring and inhaling. Lorene had been highly specific in her vision of her latest high-con restaurant/bar: a shiny, titanium-ceilinged narrow arcade, inlaid fret-patterned mosaic floors (what she described as Moroccan Neo Art Deco) with a line of low Eastern-style lacquered tables, unadorned save the exquisite but unidentical ashtrays arranged at intervals down the center. Lorene's response to the newest round of Draconian smoking laws was a defiant smoking-themed bar; a private club with the scandalous allure of the illegal vice, with a name from Ecclesiastes and a millennial affection for decadence, it was a sort of smoking speakeasy. So it was crucial to get all the trappings of the vice, such as the ashtrays, absolutely correct. Mina had been suggesting drop-bottom built-in ashtrays that could be emptied unseen and unfelt from a distance at the press of a button, or automatically at preset intervals. The question was still discussed at length between them, in the usual manner of Lorene's listening and biting her lower lip throughout, and then proffering—almost coyly—her meticulous and conclusive analysis of the issue. "Possibly," she said, nearly inaudibly. She sat on the floor at one of the tables. She waved Mina over.

"Consider this: the best smoking experience of your life, I mean the times you really loved it, really felt sexy and satisfied doing it," she said to Mina.

"I don't really smoke anymore," Mina said.

"Okay, listen." Lorene put her hand in front of Mina's eyes. "The lights are low, indirect, faintly warm—the room is crowded—but! You have a table. And you have a drink—a perfect Manhattan, let's say—and the light catches the red, it glows. And you have cigarettes and you have—what?"

"An ashtray. I thought we knew this already."

"Yes, an ashtray, but. Do you want to reach over to the center of the table and sort of toss your ash in? No, you do not. You want your own private lovely crystal or enamel ashtray that you can drag to the end of the table, to your right or to your left, so you don't have to concern yourself with dropped ashes, or horror of horrors, determining which resting cigarette is yours or the next person's." Lorene made a dramatic shuddering motion with her shoulders.

"I see your point, but then the ashtrays have to be constantly attended, because nothing is more revolting to a smoker than an ashtray full of spent butts. Then you have servers annoyingly changing ashtrays all the time, sort of reminding people how much they smoke, making them feel sheepish and ashamed. So the automatic ones work better, because smoking is private and shameful, so the key to comfort, the comfort-enabling environment, as you call it, is discretion, is it not, Lorene? And this outweighs the object-fetish factor, no matter how quaint, of a movable individual ashtray, not to mention the pilferage factor, which—"

"Ah-ha!" she enjoined, and now she actually removed her molded-celluloid blue-tinted vintage sunglasses to reveal and flash her enormous blue eyes at Mina. How long, Mina wondered, does it take to do your eyes like that? She kept glasses of one kind or another on for approximately seventy-five percent of the day. So she had her eyes perfectly made up so that when the occasion occurred wherein she needed to whip off her glasses in some grand eureka move (such as this moment about the ashtrays), the witness to the gesture—the revelation of these eyes—nearly said "Ah-ha!" right back, and was sort of nearly won before she even started talking to you.

"Ah-ha!" She started to wag a finger at Mina. "I want them to pilfer. I want to have beautiful expensive ashtrays that are distinctly of this place and I want them to be coveted and stolen. I want rich, sophisticated grown men to sneakily put them in their pockets. I want movie stars to stuff them into silk bags, scattering ashes all over pockets and purses. I want to give them the exotic thrill of a purloined thing. In fact, we won't sell them, at no price. People want them, they have to pilfer, they have to sweat. They'll become the most impressive objects on people's coffee tables. We won't say anything, neither discourage or encourage, but simply let them play out their own self-dramas."

Mina had to admit, Lorene was sort of a genius about people's desires. Secret ones. She was on constant reconnaissance from behind the blue shades, watching everyday gestures closely, seeing the longing that creates protocol and the need to break protocol. And this made her disdainful, manipulative, and very successful.

"Wait, here, take one of these," and Lorene offered her an obnoxious American cigarette, self-consciously retro in its packaging. Mina sniffed at the offered cigarette. "Look, don't raise your eyebrows, doll, they were out of my usual," she said and put the cigarette in Mina's mouth. Lorene occasionally called Mina "doll," which Mina found she enjoyed, oddly enough, quite a bit.

"So here you are, ready to smoke your cigarette. You put it in your mouth. I light it for you, you nod at me. Great. Having a cigarette lit for you is pleasant," she said.

"Not if you are chain-smoking," Mina said.

"Exactly, doll, which is why we need to have service people who are attentive but not overly so. What I mean is, the first cigarette must be lit for the customer without fail, but not the others unless it appears the customer is waiting at all for such behavior."

"I'm with you on that," Mina said, now taking a long drag.

"Take notes," Lorene said. The winding smoke gave Lorene a George Hurrel Hollywood perfection.

"Right, go ahead," Mina said, unmoving.

"It also follows that the ashtrays should be dumped by a server, not automatically, because people like to be waited on, just as they like to have their cigarette lit, et cetera. That's why they came in, let us not forget, to be waited upon. However, there is the shame at smoking so often and the customer wants to indulge unnoticed and there is the embarrassment of the service person constantly coming by and changing the tray and the horrible moment when our poor, shamed customer apologizes to the server for the bother his addiction and weakness is causing her."

"Awful," Mina shuddered, "so?"

"Well, Mina, we don't change the ashtrays until there are two butts, which is against my service rules, but since we are talking serious smokers here, and that rule was designed to cut out any judgment call on behalf of the server about the relative dirtiness of ashtrays and avoiding the long slide into casual grotesque nonstandard service, that uncrossable slippery-slope line that in this case we alter slightly, and then—"

"Yes, yes."

"We choose the most quietly subservient and inoffensive but highly attentive and observant servers, ones that are nearly invisible in their comforting perfection, angelic and flawless and gloriously impersonal."

"You mean beautiful Japanese women."

"Precisely."

Vanity and Vexation was the fourth establishment in Lorene's high-con restaurant group, Pleasure Model Enterprises. The first was Food Baroque (originally called EAT/NOT EAT, but didn't catch on until given its less prosaic moniker— Mina herself wanted it called Food Fascism, or "Eating," but that was a little too *too*, even for Pleasure Model), which initially might seem to be a sort of health food restaurant, but Lorene called it an eccentric-diet-tolerant eating environment, a gourmet restaurant that would adapt to virtually any dietary restriction; in fact, Food Baroque would plan a delicious four-course meal complete with a recommended selection from its extensive wine cellar, consisting largely of high-priced and famous older-vintage Bordeaux and Burgundies, a few sort of mammoth, macho Rhône wines, and the odd excellent, highly allocated, and difficult-to-find California boutique wines. Since the wine was matched so specifically to their personal menu, most people gratefully went along with the selection. This was where Pleasure Model made its profits, and that margin allowed Lorene to reserve only two seatings a night, so the kitchen could actually adapt to the many different menus. Mina spent her first year working for Lorene tirelessly and meticulously entering the highly specific and esoteric dietary restrictions into the computer (all extremely confidential) and creating client histories so regulars would only have to make a reservation and Mina would see their complete restrictive history listed before her. She developed the current Food Baroque system: Producer and Young Wife call for reservation, two weeks in advance minimum, and confirmed on Amex (at a charge of $50 a person if the reservation was canceled with less than a week's notice). Producer specifies no red meat, low cholesterol, under twenty percent saturated fat (entered as XRM, –C, <20%sF). Wife is 600k, –CB, XS, +O3 (no more than six hundred calories, low carbohydrates, no sugar, and high omega-three oils). Or any combination thereof. The clients were devoted and, Mina realized, quite unpleasant people, alternately deeply paranoid (constant rumors surfaced after Food Baroque was a sensation that they ignored the restrictions altogether, and in fact the food tasted so good because the chef put a stick of butter in everything), and deeply grateful, with young starlets weeping with joy and holding Mina's hand, as at long last they could have their cake and not have to purge it as well. Her excellent management of FB earned Lorene's loyalty forever, and certainly gave Mina license now, in the wake of their success, occasionally to be hours late, or be there but not be there, and Lorene accommodated Mina's eccentricities as Mina accommodated the eccentricities of Food Baroque customers. Mina had grown to hate FB, and had fantasies about the days when the fundamental thing about food was taste, finito. It was in fact essential to Lorene and Mina's success to remember that every success had to be contradicted and revised in order to maintain itself, each extreme had to contain its own contradiction, each virtue its vice, each style its own mannered counterstyle. Lorene realized, in another eureka moment, that certain loyal customers used to sneak in the back alley for a cigarette between courses of guiltless, organic "lite" cuisine. She created a downstairs "private" smoking room, a secret lounge with elegant banquettes and beautiful service persons wherein a customer could bum a cigarette (even call in his favorite brand with his dietary restrictions) and smoke in privacy, and only in view of other guilty smokers. Only smokers knew of the room, so spouses could be fooled about the reformation of smokers, and the clients could enjoy their weakness with no shame. Phillipe Stark disposable toothbrushes were even provided in the secret room's secret bathroom, so the telltale breath could be eliminated before returning to the main dining room. So chic and popular this little room became that many notorious power deals were struck there, and some ambitious mongering types even cynically feigned being smokers just to get in, until Lorene had to pick and choose the "right" smokers. She spun this secret room into its own place, Dead Animals and Single Malts (with the added attraction of wild exotic-game meat such as buffalo filet mignon, New Zealand ostrich prosciutto, and free-range alligator carpaccio), and as successful as that was, and well ahead of the current macho scotch, cigar, and "meat" craze, it never had the cachet of the Room at Food Baroque, the sassy defiance of the secret cigarette. It closed after the recent smoking laws went into effect. Mina saw Vanity and Vexation as another attempt to recapture the Room, and didn't disguise her indifference, although undoubtedly it would have great success.

Mina's favorite establishment of Lorene's and the true gem and heart of Pleasure Model Enterprises, at least in Mina's view, was the Gentleman's Club, which opened a year and a half after Food Baroque. It was the place both of them spent most of their time, Mina working the floor nearly every night the first year, and Lorene nearly always starting or ending her days there. The place was conceived, initially, as a men's club, a forties service-man's-style club, though ersatz even as such: a serviceman's club but as imagined in fifties movies about wartime service-man's clubs. Gentlemanly recreation with the opposite gen-der—that sort of thing. The idea was hire pretty girls and dress them in slightly undersized forties vintage dresses. Give them names like Shirley and Annette. Lorene required them to be about fifteen pounds over the standard L.A. beauty—she wanted hips and curves, retro bodies. Initially it worked that way, only men allowed, and lots of girls to wait on them and have bright conversation, ordering them sidecars and Manhat-tans and old-fashioneds, Harvey Wallbangers and salty dogs. No boutique bourbons or single-batch tequilas or single malts. It was quite a successful place, but Lorene had to compromise and allow women customers, finally. Women, then, ironically, became the most loyal customers (or, actually, members—everyone who entered had to join for ten dollars to enjoy the recreation and refreshments of the club—this also allowed Lorene to skirt the smoking laws, as it was a private club, and members could smoke and eat and talk in peace). Women loved to chat up the "girls"—this had a quaint, faintly outré sort of kink to it, women as fifties-stylized forties servicemen, missing the company of the sweet and lovely chubby woman. Thus the Gentleman's Club sprung its own cooler opposite, as "Gentleman's Club," with more women members than men. It was there they were to meet, the following evening, at the long bar, when Mina again turned up several hours late.

Lorene was waiting, smoking at the bar. Mina sat on the stool next to her. The bar was packed, and Lorene shook her head.

"I thought you only saw Scott one weekend a month."

"Well, Scott, yes. Sorry."

"David did call and I did cover for you."

"Great. Cover. You're top shelf," Mina said. "Drink?"

"Ray." Lorene gestured at Ray (real name Brandon, or Brendan, or was it Branden?—but Lorene couldn't have that).

Ray hand-polished his glasses. "What'll it be today, girls?" Lorene also specified that staff refer to women (even in the vocative) as "girls," never as "ladies," "miss," or (God forbid!) "women."

"I'll have a Norman Maine on the rocks," Mina said.

"I'll have a Holly Martins," Lorene said. Ray filled two glasses with club soda and placed them on the bar in front of them, as he always did, no matter what they ordered.

"Look, I don't mind covering for you, just let me know ahead of time."

"Sorry, I meant to get here sooner, but I ended up walking home and then I couldn't bring myself to go in," Mina said.

"It's gone on a bit, this Scott thing. Really, it's your business."

"Yes, Scott. A bit. My business."

"I'm not even going to address this walking business."

"I like to walk."

"Someone might say you are scared to drive."

"I'm not. I prefer walking."

"I think someone might say that anyone with as complicated a personal life as you have might not be able to afford the luxury of preferring to walk places."

"Lorene."

"But I'm not even going to mention it."

Mina had been seeing Scott regularly for about six months. Lorene was the only one who knew. She told her one day, "I need you to cover me one weekend a month." Lorene said, "Yes?" And Mina said, "His name is Scott." Lorene just said, "Scott. Scott. Well, with a name like Scott, he must be lonely." So Mina would let her think it was still Scott. Not tell her about Max. She had secrets now within her secrets. Secrets from her secrets.

"Poor Scott," Lorene said.

Yes, poor Scott. Mina had met him in a hotel bar that seemed to have been there forever and was always deserted, her sort of place. It was in walking distance of the Gentleman's Club, and one of those places she meandered by in the early stages of her "walking places." She sat there, taking a break from the restaurant to get a real drink. A three o'clock on a Saturday afternoon drink, something shadowed and filmish and seductive, the perversion of the sun outside. She needed a cigarette, and a man, obviously. One day after another of working, and she couldn't bear it. She walked in and ordered an Irish whisky, neat.

A young man was sitting at the bar. When her sweater slipped off her stool, he picked it up for her. He had on a suit, an actual suit, with a tie and cuff links and a jacket. He smiled and handed her her sweater.

"Thank you," she said, and smiled at him.

It seemed such an archaic, nice thing to do.

He smiled and nodded and went back to his stool. She felt warm from the drink and wanted another. The young man in the suit gestured at the bartender, pointing at his glass and hers. The bartender probably had a real name, like Sam, because he was so old. It occurred to Mina that she liked bartenders to be a lot older than she. She had to make a note of this for Gentleman's Club. She smiled at the young man and gestured him over. He was drinking a gold-hued liquid in a highball glass filled with ice that certainly had to be scotch.

"May I join you?" he said and she nodded. They sat there saying nothing, sipping, staring at the bartender. She could discern the unmistakable peaty-grassy scotch smell from his glass and his mouth when he spoke. She wanted to hear him talk.

"You're visiting?" she said.

He explained he was visiting his daughter, two years old. His wife had left him several months earlier, and now he came to L.A. once a month to visit his kid.

"You're from New York?" she asked. He was. But not originally. He was from Georgia. His name was Scott Winter. Married his sweetheart. Became an investment banker. Worked long hours. She left him. He was in a suit, postvisit to the indifferent kid, hapless and having a few.

"A banker," she said, "in a suit."

"Is that bad?" he asked with complete earnestness. "I ask because I don't know. It must seem odd, here in Los Angeles."

He was very slender, nearly petite. He was not greatlooking, but handsome in an inoffensive, smooth-cheeked, high-school kind of way, nice-shaped face, sort of ridiculous pink cheeks and voluptuous mouth, all a bit disconcerting combined with the dark circles under the eyes. He was one of those guys who would go from looking twenty-five to forty-five overnight.

"Were you very popular in high school?" she asked.

"Well, high school was a long time ago," he said.

"Yeah, you were. That's okay. You really work for a bank. Sort of get up and go to work every day in a suit. How about that." He looked at her oddly.

"I'm sorry, I'm bothering you," he said, and his face was blank and sad.

"You're not, Scott. Really not. I'm just talking. It's my way, I'm sorry, I don't mean anything I say," Mina said. "I'm not making fun of you. I'm making fun of me." He again looked at her oddly. She realized he was a bit struck, and it was amazingly attractive to Mina.

They sat quietly, mid-distance staring. Two people drinking in a dark bar while the sun burned brightly outside. He didn't leave. They sipped their drinks. She leaned her head in close to him.

"Scott," she said. He looked at her.

"Scott, I love the way a man's mouth tastes after he's been drinking scotch.

"Scott." She put her hand on his sleeve. She touched his tie. "I'd like to undress you. Your tie and your cuff links." Scott opened his mouth to speak and then closed it. When they had closed the door to his hotel room, he fastened the chain lock. After she took her clothes off, he touched her with reverent slowness, as if she might run out the door any second.

"I think you're beautiful," he said. She couldn't wait to pull him on top of her. She didn't want his dutiful body kisses. She pulled him on top of her and, putting her hands on the backs of his thighs, she pulled him inside her. He came pretty quickly, and she did not even approach coming. But the thrusts, the long wet and the deep fast of them, made the world basic and elemental to her. She let him stroke her back for a long time afterward, and listened to him talk about his divorce and how his daughter didn't seem familiar to him. She listened to him talk about the long hours he worked and she played with his cock until he wanted to have sex again, and she said to herself she liked it short and uncomplicated. When she left she agreed to meet him in the same place a month from then.

It had felt as though she were watching this unfold from somewhere else. That someone wrote all this down beforehand for them to recite.

That first time, when the dusk air hit her face on the street, a heat blast of tropical stillness, she felt invincible and lonely. But her loneliness was at a distance, something she could control and look at, specific and acute. It had a reason and a logic. She already longed for next month. Months slid by and she found these meetings (dates, trysts, assignations—what should she call them?) could go on indefinitely, isolated, contained, like a secret cigarette in some back-stairs room.

Max was not merely an escalation of this, not simply a revision. Max was the time bomb, the flash point of doomed relations, the Florence and Normandy of her Secret Life. Max was not contained and isolated. Max was her husband's oldest and best friend.

Lorene ordered another drink. "A *Lost Weekend*," she said. Mina looked at her.

"Another, Mina?" Ray asked.

"I'll have *An Affair to Remember*. A double." Ray obliged

with the club soda and the lime squeezes. She sipped her soda and watched Lorene smoke.

"Do you think if you are semi-involved with two people, or three, or four—let's say twenty-five percent engagement with each . . ."

"Yes?"

"Does that mean you are fully engaged? In the aggregate?"

"No."

"Or is it just the same twenty-five percent over and over, and nothing ever even reaches thirty percent?"

"What?"

"Skip it."

"Take the night off. Take a walk. Take care of David. I'll cover things here," Lorene said, smiling and patting her hand.

The Metro section was spread open and out of order from when her husband, Mark, had thrown it at the refrigerator earlier in the morning. Lisa picked it up, smoothing its creases, just glancing at headlines but not getting too involved until she had her coffee and had set up Alex and Alisa with their shows and the saltines with grape jelly.

He had trouble with mornings.

Lisa rarely missed reading the paper. She read it, at least the front section and the Metro section, every day. She had to, it seemed. The Metro section covered the local human disasters from the hundreds of suburban-sprawl cities, Spanish named, all inter-paso-changeable. El- and Santa- and Del- and La- and Costa-named places. But the freeways too, lately, always there, impossible for Lisa to place precisely. Living in the city, you know the freeways you use, and to read of the others—whole other worlds right there, apparently—made her feel the huge vastness of the place, something so intangible when she went to the Safeway, or even the west side to clean houses. The Santa Ana, the San Diego, the San Gabriel, the Pomona—freeways named for their origins or destinations like rivers. But how could that be, a freeway ending? Wasn't the very point that they became an endless, seamless circle? Or the names that seemed to promise things—Garden Grove Freeway, Artesia Freeway, Century Freeway. Harbor Freeway, Golden State Freeway.

He had a headache, of course. He had to do a lot of drinking to just unwind and get some sleep. And when Lisa woke at five, she paused for a second before she woke Mark up. She looked at him in bed next to her, watched him sleep. He had long brown hair, which he didn't braid, as she suggested, so as he slept it tangled and knotted. He had a heavy, noisy man's way of sleep-breathing, as if he managed to aggravate the air even unconsciously, a constant announcement or battle. A labor, that's what they called it. His breathing labored, even in his sleep. And that word, *labor,* made Lisa feel sorry for him. She felt bad, actually, that he would now wake and have to go to the job site and labor—climb things and hammer things and do the things that made his hands swollen at the end of the day. He hated it so much. She, on the other hand, didn't mind cleaning the house, or Lorene's house, or any of the houses she did. Sometimes her back hurt and she couldn't believe how much laundry and shopping and dishes still had to be done after she had done so much. But it kept her focused and she liked having things to do. Poor Mark, though, he really hated it.

Lisa started to read about local disappearances. There was the child found dead in a trash pail. The story about the one held captive in a basement. Found was harder to take, usually so tortured they may as well be dead, so horrendously damaged they were. But what got Lisa were not the found victims but the missing children. The victims-to-be, certainly, awaiting their stories. The dopey school picture reprinted—Lisa scanned the awkward smiles with the new, still-jagged-edged adult teeth just grown in, the strange school picture with matte wash color backdrops, the ribbon at an innocent angle on the head. Couldn't there be something in the faces that indicated the horrors to come? That they would be chosen for the worst, most horrific random disasters? But there was nothing in these faces that made them any different from any other kids. No different from Alex and Alisa, no predicting their victimhood.

He still had his trim, smooth-skinned athletic body. Sometimes, when he came to bed stoned and only a little drunk, she would rub his back, massage him, and it felt nice to touch the smooth, hard muscles. Watching him sleep, with one arm bent under the pillow under his head, she noticed how his bicep muscle swelled, distinct and strong, the angle making a sculpted furrow underneath the muscle and a pleasing curve on the top to his shoulder. How she used to ache to see it, how she liked to curl in there and feel surrounded by strong maleness, cared for. How amazingly hard and different from her own this man's body felt. She was so certain this was what she needed and wanted. All this hard flesh around her. And she would stroke his muscles and feel girlish and safe. She grew ever softer and he grew ever harder.

Lisa didn't let the kids watch the TV news. That's why she turned to the paper. No TV news with Alex and Alisa nearby. No—they watched their *Little Mermaid* video, or *Anastasia*, and she must read of the world around them, a world of hunted and hated children. A world in every way hostile to children. Mindy Brown, seven. Missing three days. Last seen at a playground. In a red sweatshirt with a hood and a zipper, and with her *101 Dal-matians* backpack. Items to find in mud somewhere, blood-stained and zip-locked in plastic bags. She just knew what came next—canvass the neighborhood, because it's only bad—right? Lisa knew from reading every day how it went, the search, the increasing futility, then the body part found, and the story became matching decomposed bodies to missing babies. Then the grisly back-telling of events. The rope burns indicate the time of asphyxiation. Evidence of penetration. Struggle indi-cated before water filled lungs. One shoe missing. Strange lac-erations across shoulders. Head injuries indicating bludgeoning with perhaps a pipe or a crowbar. The technical language attempted a clinical precision, but it was pornography. Lisa hated to read it, could not stop reading it, couldn't help but visu-alize events. Dylan Simonson. Age five. Lisa knew what five was. Alex and Alisa were five. Five was animal crackers and full-throttle energy, finally with an agile coordination that encour-aged them to be more independent, to play by themselves at times, to feel a sense of littleness as liberation—maybe the real-ization that small people can do things grown-ups cannot, a first wave of self-esteem, even able to trick Dad and call Mom "dumb." She had just left him in the car for five minutes. Or she just sent him ten feet away to the gum ball machine. He was playing on the slides and I was just sitting here talking to Mrs. Williams. I looked around and he was gone. One negligent moment and then it's get the dental records.

Sometimes she caught Mark looking at the three of them like he'd wandered into the wrong house. That is the word, *caught*, he looked caught, and you could read it as something else, but she knew better.

Lisa began to read less of anything but these stories. She got to know them so well that if a body was found she knew which kids were still missing, which child it probably would turn out to be. She had a vague feeling that this wasn't good, thinking so much about these things. Or maybe it was crucial she thought about them. She remembered when they used to put pictures of missing children on milk cartons. So America would wake up in the morning, and there next to their Wheaties and multigrain toast would be the face of some certainly dead child, hopelessly missing for years, computer altered to simulate age. Lisa supposed the milk companies finally wised up and realized that these death cartons were not the most pleasing packaging for their products. She remembered the joke Mark made to her when they saw a small child wandering around the mall by himself, so absorbed in a toy he turned around to find himself separated from Mom. "Look, Lisa," he'd said with a cryptic smile, "a milk carton kid." It was true, the solo child was a potential candidate for the milk carton. But those milk cartons on the table—maybe off-putting, but maybe a reminder to the kiddies: Hey, be careful. Hansel and Gretel. To the parents: Pay attention to every second. No second chances in this forever larger and unfamiliar freewayed world.

Second Road Stop:
Between Arizona and New Mexico

"Why do I hate the ocean? Well, I don't, I just don't have the sentimental fetish for it that all these people do. As if the ocean on the one side and the desert on the other sort of justifies whatever lies between." Lorene smokes her long cigarette and will not take off her sunglasses. We sit in a bar in a town halfway between Flagstaff and Santa Fe. We sit in the afternoon light and she will not take off her sunglasses.

"The sun is our enemy, don't you know, Mina, beware always of the sun. Relentless, inexhaustible summer is no way to live your life." I eat a hamburger. She watches. I can feel her hunger like a wave behind her glasses. I eat with gusto, but not too fast. I sense her watching my every move. She keeps speaking as if we were having a conversation.

"It's important to live in a place that is affected by seasons. Where time is measured in weather. Where there are constant reminders that your approaching death is inescapable. You know, leaves falling, that sort of thing." I slurp on my Coke. She lights another cigarette.

"Mud slides don't count. Disasters, fires, unusual weather systems don't count. Earthquakes don't count. They are just random, a kind of meaningless natural hysteria. Earthquakes, when you grow up in California, they are like an E-ticket ride at Disneyland, a joke, a way to make the nonnatives come forth and identify themselves." The afternoon light on her white face makes her look celluloid, as if she could shift the whole world to black-and-white. Michael said there is nothing more beautiful than white, white skin because it is so unforgiving, so bruisable, and the person inside seems only barely covered. To me her cheek looks cool and poreless, not at all trembly and translucent. But she may have been different then. Or maybe he could see through skin.

"Oh, honey, you're upset." Lorene leans toward me as if she could see me only now, as if she had just walked into the room.

I feel nothing, but there must have been a sort of look on my face. I stare out the window. A large woman is trying to get her stuff into her tote bag. Kids' clothes and hairbrush and cigarettes all spilling out. She has blond hair cut close on the sides and left long in back. Her toes press over the edges of her sandals and the nails are not deep red but lollipop red. Her son is tiny beside her, pulling at her. I keep staring at the fat part of the backs of her legs, the part where the skin puckers whitely and it looks as if no nerves are there, that if you touched her flesh she wouldn't know.

"Lorene," I say.

"Yes?"

"I think I made a huge mistake."

"Oh, dear. Do you want to go back, doll?"

"No, no, no. I don't mean leaving L.A."

"What do you mean?"

"Oh, Lorene. Oh, God. I've made an awful mistake."

Lorene frowns. She's not wearing any lipstick. First time ever.

Three Weeks from Leaving

Mina ran the dining room floor for the long lunch shift at Food Baroque. A usual exhaustion of mishaps: strangers agitated and demanding. The bookings changing constantly. The regulars who had to be appeased. The waitresses who had to be constantly reminded of so many tiny details. Mina greeted people

with a surface smile and was grateful for the still-heavy protocol of restaurants. There was a structure and an order, and
everybody knew it. I say hello. You say hello back. I ask how
you are. You smile, nod, and announce the name the booking
is under. I take you to a table, you thank me. We know this.
First, I offer you a drink. We serve the drinks from the right. We
serve food from the left. I show you the label of the wine. I
place the cork in front of you. I offer you the taste. This is the
way it is done. I fill glasses of the women clockwise from the
host, then the men, then I fill the host's glass. This structure is
understood between us, even though I've never seen you
before. There is a grace and a comfort in these rules. Mina
found refuge in them, a kind of beauty. She thought of it, pon-
dered the rules of service, the order necessary to create pleasure. People still feel, however superficially, part of some
coherent common culture where gestures among strangers are
understood. She missed actually waiting on people. She loved
marking the tables between courses with the appropriate silverware. She loved serving the women first, whisking crumbs
off the tables with a sliver of metal designed for such niceties.
It was about pleasure, the rules of pleasure and service, and
Mina marveled at this, and lately inserted little torques in the
protocol, not destroying them but emphasizing them by playing with the edges. She would make a tiny personal comment
on the wine, or give a piece of silverware an extra twirl as she
placed it to mark a table for the next course. She would hold
eye contact a second longer than appropriate when asked what
the wait for a table was, and then give a minutely precise
answer with a deadpan earnestness. She could create ironic
service, a swerve to the unexpected that would succeed only
because everything was already intact and flawless; only play if

a space exists. And there could be no mistaking that the swerves came from art rather than sloppiness or ignorance. She would never incorrectly serve food from the right and clear from the left—that would be a meaningless erosion of order. Because there was a kind of beauty in this sort of mutually observed propriety. It was pleasing to have gestures to read, rules to respect, structures to subvert.

She had the weekly staff meeting today at Gentleman's Club. Billie Jean, Nancy, Roxanne, Annette (not their real names) were instructed in the rules of service by Lorene as Mina looked on, nodding. The same things over and over like a prayer, tiny, seemingly insignificant details that architected Lorene's vision of pleasure. She was so confident in her vision, it hardly mattered whether it was right or not. It *was* right. Then Lorene went over the schedule, with all of the girls' astrological charts in hand. No earth signs on the floor with fire signs. The planets dictated these combinations, and that, along with the audition demands of the actress/servers, made the schedule challenging. Mina was left to the task of reconciling all this: the back of the house, the front of the house, the sun, the moon, the pilot season. After she finished and discharged the girls to the evening shift, she had a look at the reservation book. A hopelessly overbooked seven o'clock seating. A wishful booking at nine for a two-hour turn. Not likely. She left the impending disasters of the half-hour waits at the bar and the nearly threatening, polite assertiveness of rich beautiful people who "didn't want to wait a moment longer, please" to the night manager, Billie Jean, and said she would be at home if needed.

On the way, she had to squeeze in Max, briefly. The walk home separated things.

She again stood outside, staring at the house she lived in, a

Mildred Pierce-y sort of bungalow, its stucco walls surrounded by palm trees. Palm trees, palm trees. Dr. Seuss, branchless, Betty Boop, shadeless, wind-bent, transplanted palm "trees." No matter how long she had lived here, no matter how many summers she had spent here as a child, she never failed to become momentarily unnerved by palm trees. They seemed to say, This isn't a real place where things count, this is exotic, this is tropical, this is a vacation! And she got a kind of thrill from it, living here was a sort of faux living, it's what gave her so much license with time. Southern California ambivalence that was too bright to be ennui. Too palm-treed. Natives were not supposed to get a thrill from a palm tree. It was just a tree. It could be a fir or an evergreen or an oak. She strove to find the tiny details that illuminated the vast differences between the rest of Los Angeleans and herself, and, especially lately, between herself and David. What was she trying to convince herself of, with this little game? Anyone scrutinized in this way would seem hopelessly strange. When she finally reached the vantage point outside David's office, she became entranced with watching him look intently at his computer screen. She watched him take a sip of tea (she drank coffee and didn't even understand tea), his eyes not wavering from the blue-green light of the screen, her eyes not wavering from him.

She entered the kitchen and saw that David had washed all the dishes. He was very tidy. She has had her moments, but they've been unpredictable and, generally, David has kept things in order. He stepped into the kitchen when she opened the refrigerator.

"How was work?" he asked. She shrugged and opened a cardboard to-go container. She ate in front of the open refrigerator. "Hey," he said, "you want to order a movie?" She nodded, chewing, and he approached her. He put his hand on her shoulder. "I'm not getting anywhere on these rewrites. I'm sick of it." David was finishing a tenth rewrite of a script about white, rural, Luddite, fundamentalist terrorists who plan to blow up the White House.

"It's timely" was all he would really say about it. Whenever she described the plot as being about white, rural, Luddite, fundamentalist terrorists, he corrected her. "It's not about the terrorists. It's about the hero who thwarts them." But he often didn't say more than that. He was weary of it, as he was weary of all the scripts he wrote and rewrote. When she first met him he was an art history student. He was someone who used to trace his fingertips, with a dreamy shyness, along the hollow at the back of her knee.

"I'm sorry," she said, mouth full of moo shu pork. It was actually all vegetarian. Almost moo shu pork. It was made of seitan.

"Isn't that what they use to make wicker chairs?" David joked. It was soba and tempeh and seitan. Fibrous mystery food from the East. Almost tasted like real food, faux moo shu pork. She spooned it in. She had the postcoital munchies. She had the postmeandering famishes. Wretched, she thought, and ravenous.

"You know, we could actually eat dinner," he said.

"I plan to," she said, still chewing. Mina could eat a tremendous amount of food. She really enjoyed eating. Also, it felt vaguely defiant. So anti-Lorene. A woman of appetites. She laughed at the young waitresses/actresses working at the restaurants, watching them control their eating, fasting and constantly rebuilding their castles of deprivation. They had neophyte eating disorders. Hers was so elaborated, so long contemplated, that it full-circled to the appearance of a normative eating pattern. Yes, a retro affectation—a woman who eats. That kind of self-obsession was an art, a silent, pure art performed and appreciated only by one's self. She wasn't defiant enough to be fat, though. There was a little fullness around the hips, a smoothing of edges that had occurred over the last two or three years. Over-twenty-five metabolic slowing. The inevitable decline begun. But of late, of Max, she liked this softness around the hips. It felt sexy somehow. A concession to the immoderate and sensual. Female and decadent, even. She planned, at some liberated later point, to be able to romanticize her fat, fetishize it. But then there was cellulite. Then there was the drooping of large breasts. Sagging. Technically called ptosis. It was a syndrome, a medical problem to be fixed, don't you know. A pathology, surely. The pencil test. If you placed a pencil under your breast and it stayed there, if the leaning, sagging breast actually held the pencil there, you failed the pencil test. Fallen buttocks, too. Stretch marks. Lapsed uterus, for God's sake.

Mina stopped eating.

Of course, there was always Dr. Mencer, Lorene's plastic surgeon. The pencil test, what sadistic misogynist came up with that one? But it could be fixed, nothing was irrevocable. All was curable. Good old Dr. Mencer.

She ate another mouthful.

"I suppose we could order in," David said. She nodded. "Sushi," he said.

"I'm bored—in a deep, profound, practically hysterical way—with sushi," Mina said, "and besides, they give you the dregs for to-go orders."

"They do not. It's the same sushi."

"Dregs. Ends. The unlucky pieces. Unwanted, bad luck, cat food pieces."

"That's in your head," David said. Mina made a mental note that David needed to be drunk to go down on her, but he'd eat sushi from three days ago. He'd eat it warm and wilted, he'd eat it from Super Sushi Surprise if he had to.

"It's yesterday's. The edges are curled. It's salmonella and mercury drenched. It's a petri dish. It's a penicillin experiment," she said.

"Oh, stop. You don't get salmonella from fish."

"Well, then trichinosis. Or trignomisis. The trich," she said, "didn't you hear about the Brentwood housewife who got herpes from a piece of slightly used anago? A piece of previously owned maguro?"

"I heard it was genital warts. From take-out sushi."

"Right," she said.

"Pizza, okay."

"I'll order it," Mina said. She pulled open the drawer by the phone. It was full of paper menus.

"Hey, you got some mail today," David said from the bathroom.

"I did?"

"I almost forgot. A postcard. It's by the phone," he shouted. She listened to the shower running. He took showers, she took baths. She noted that, repeating it to herself. Added it to the list compiled for some unknown purpose. He takes showers. Tea. Ignores palm trees. He's tidy. He drives.

The postcard was a photo of the Andalusian countryside. The card said only one word, "LEFT," in block capital letters and was unsigned. The postmark was San Francisco.

David appeared, a towel jauntily tied around his hips. Mina

admired his body, damp, tan, and lean, and the hair on his legs and arms and chest in artful wet swirls. The towel tied around the hips. The way the drops of water found all his hollows.

"Who sent the card?" he said.

"Don't know," she said.

"It's got a San Francisco postmark," David said. David had checked the postmark. He was pondering her mail. She was almost touched, almost excited. She put her finger on his belly. Dragged her finger to his hipbone. The skin was damp and warm. She traced the outline of the hip to where it reached the towel. She could hear him exhale. She thought, I should, I should. She put her hands on his hips and angled them forward, toward her. He did nothing, he was pliant, and she didn't look at him but bent from the waist to where the hair started to curl and leaned downward. She put her lips there. It felt soft and wet, and when she licked she could feel a trembly sort of movement. His hands were on her shoulders, and he started to pull her shirt up along her back as she bent into him. She grabbed his wrists. He let her. She held his hands out to his sides away from them both. She pushed the towel down with her face. She felt him looking down at her. She pulled her face back a little, closing her eyes, imagining what she looked like, her lips moving on his cock, her hair stranded on her jaw and forehead. She saw them both, her mouth attaining a sort of mesmerized rhythm, and the muscles in his legs and abdomen tightening. She heard his urgent breaths. Then she heard him sigh and some seconds later she felt him shiver. She thought of Max coming, earlier, and then she felt David come. No one should know these things about her. She wouldn't let herself think about it. David held her for balance and then unwound. She was glad his body felt so heavy, glad being with Max made him a body again, made him unfamiliar and sexy. He smiled at her, shaking his wet hair. Anyone, *anyone*, would find him appealing. He leaned to kiss her.

"The pizza will be here soon. Don't you think we should call the Videorama?" she said, pulling back from the kiss.

They rented a Gary Cooper movie. Movie choices—rental choices, actually, because they never saw movies in the theater anymore, that would have required effort and actually leaving the house and possible contact with strangers—Mina and David often didn't agree on. Mina had her obsessional way with movies. She liked to see all of a certain actor's films, or a director's, or a related batch of films. She would want only postwar melodrama. A William Wyler festival. Or only William Holden. Or postaccident Montgomery Clift. Only British-produced Hitchcock. A Dorothy Malone/Gloria Grahame/"sort of slutty" festival. Films were an organic, coherent whole, with categories and patterns. She saw them connected to the world and to each other. It comforted her to exhaustively track a single career, the rise, the fall. It was the drama outside the drama, and the movies were the artifacts that remained. Her father had filled in obscure production details, quoted lines. He would make jokes, inward metacomments that spoke to their organic movie world, their exclusive and idiosyncratic expertise.

"What's going on?" her father would say, watching *Red River.* "What's Wayne doing, he's in a rush because he left all those people on the stagecoach." Mina would laugh at his joke, because she had seen *Stagecoach,* too. She would say, Well, they better get to Missouri before the army realizes Matt is AWOL. Very good, kid, he would say, and she thought she knew the whole world watching movies with her father. And mostly old, and mostly American. She liked to imagine living in 1952 and seeing these lady melodramas. She imagined herself housewifed and weeping. Or old war and baseball movies—they made her nostalgic, made her homesick for a time she never even lived through. And she thought she could see what her father was like, at seventeen, watching *From Here to Eternity.* Imagining him watching those movies for the first time made him seem more like a real person, less like someone's father. It made her feel a funny kind of sad affection for him. She saw him leaving the theater and she tried to guess what seventeen-year-old Jack felt, whether he thought he was more like Burt Lancaster or more like Frank Sinatra. As she grew older, old films gave her pleasure as the secret heart not just of her father, but of the world, collective pseudomemory of American innocence, Norman Rockwell but more sordid and ironic because the medium wasn't static—as contexts changed the actual films became ironic and winking. They moved from American to Americana. She knew Gary Cooper spilled his guts to the House Un-American Activities Committee. That was why his brave American heroes were fun to watch. She knew Clift was gay—it made his ambivalent, helpless shrugs all the more resonant. Mina had so many movie reference points in her head, as many as the memories of her own life, it seemed, and they became nearly equally weighted, her memories of her actual life and her memories of the movies she had seen. Was there finally that much difference? She sometimes thought that if someone saw all the movies she had seen, the number of times she had seen them and in the order she had seen them, that person might know exactly who she was. That couldn't really be true, but it was half true, it felt that crucial, as if her identity were a collection of references.

She watched Cooper's long eyelashes and baseball swagger

as he rubbed his bad arm and let Barbara Stanwyck talk circles around him. David wanted to see a seventies action film. Mina wanted anything—anything at all—with James Mason. They settled for an easy one. They compromised on a film they had both seen dozens of times.

"Sometimes a film we haven't seen before seems like so much effort," Mina said.

"Daunting and risky," David said. He commented constantly. He had to—they'd seen it too many times to actually be engaged. They now sought the supracritique. The odd detail you missed the first eight times you saw it. The depth of repetition. The continuity gaffes. The way the timing of the dialogue had rhythm. Sometimes Mina thought if you watched one movie enough, it could mean anything. It became a funnel for the entire universe. Besides, it was the most talking they would do all day.

David, the technician, the analyst, said, "You can't get away with dialogue like that anymore. Too much talking."

"But it's good still."

"Yeah. It is. You can't, though."

Mina nodded, not turning from the eyelashes. The black and white and gray luminous movie eyes. She knew Cooper's eyes were cerulean blue, translucent and denim-flecked and cold, an impossible manly American Blue, the way she knew Rita Hayworth's Gilda nails in black-and-white had to be a platonic perfect sex-sinister Red.

"Now you have to have less dialogue. It has to be careful and tricky, though. It can't be too obvious. The lovers fight, then say, 'I can't live without you.' Or they're making love, and she sighs and says, 'You bastard.' It has to go like that," he said, looking at the TV.

Mina, eyes on Cooper, said, "Yeah. I think that's called irony, David." And it came out more sarcastic and mean than she intended. Cooper was shrugging, in that "It seems to me but what do I know" kind of common, noble way. Cooper was starting to irritate her.

"You're a snob," David said quietly, looking at the screen.

It's funny that she often forgave things in other people that irritated her in David. She fingered the Andalusian "LEFT" postcard folded in her pocket. Left of what? Why Andalusia? She'd have to call the hospital tomorrow. She felt moody and impatient.

"We should have rented *Only Angels Have Wings*. Rita Hayworth. Cary Grant. And that actress with the oddly pitched voice."

"Who?" David said.

"She's wearing slacks. These great slacks."

"Jean Peters."

LEFT. Of course. It was left *from*, not *of*.

David cracked a beer open triumphantly. "Oh, I have to have lunch with my agent tomorrow."

"On Saturday?"

David shrugged.

"Well, I have to work tomorrow night at the club, so I guess I won't see you."

David nodded. He took another sip of beer and watched the screen.

"Jean Arthur. Not Jean Peters, for Christ's sake."

"I love Gary Cooper," David said.

"Jean Arthur, David."

Mina took a long, hot bubble bath. She stared at the parts of her body that poked out from the bubbles. She extended a leg to wash seductively. A commercial, it reminded her of. Her leg looked great, all bubble-dripping against the tile. She tried to forget pencil tests. She wrapped a towel turban-style around her head. She emptied the tub. She stopped on the way to the bedroom at the door to David's office. He was at his computer again. The room was completely dark except for the sickly green-blue aura of the screen.

Mina stood watching David. David watched the screen, which contained a small screen within the screen that watched some other guy's computer, unattended and unmoving. Free-streaming live-feed video. Sometimes you could watch him at his computer. Sometimes he left and you could just watch his computer.

"I can watch him for minutes at a time," David said.

"I do other things. I eat my lunch, I talk on the phone," Mina said.

"He stares at his screen. Does nothing. Occasionally he works the keyboard, but mostly he watches," David said, eyes fixed.

"I walk around. I see people. I smell things. I take baths, David."

"I like to watch real life, a stranger's life, in real time. There is unlimited space, so the most atomic details are available. The most micro moments get play. Everything is attended."

"You know what I pray for?" Mina said.

"It's just different things that engage you, not that things engage you less."

"I pray for the day I pick up the paper and they discover that the Internet is a big failure and everyone is wrong and nobody wants to use it anymore."

"It's not that you get more information shoved at you. It's

just different. And you have to figure out what you want. You have to be more accurate in your desires."

"They would say, 'Oh, boy, remember the Internet? What a fad that was.' And people who hated it would be congratulated. 'Boy, you guys were smart not to bother with that, how did ya know?'"

"Infinitesimal things can have as much pull as massive things. Things are not privileged in the same way. Eccentricity is encouraged."

"I hate the fucking Internet."

"You can bet on that making no difference at all. You can bet everything on that."

"Oh look, he's moving. What—look, I think he just—did you see that, David?"

"That's nothing. Let's go to live-streaming accidents."

"How can they be live? How do they know an accident will happen?"

"There are certain street corners, one in L.A., one in New York, and of course, the best one is in Athens, where accidents happen up to three or four times a day. These live cams just surveil those corners. See?"

"But there is no accident."

"But it's all an accident. This is guaranteed preaccident footage."

"Have you ever actually seen a live accident on this site?"

"Actual live, at the actual occurrence, or replayed highlight, postlive?"

"Actual-live live."

"Actually, no."

Saturday His-and-Her Perversities

The week before it was the "trashy" lingerie superstore on a famously dilapidated boulevard. Today it was Mitterrand's Mistress, an exclusive European hosiery-only boutique. Mina bought cashmere tights, guaranteed to let you wear skirts through the most frigid days of winter. They were the most expensive hose in the store, even more than the hand-stitched lace-topped stay-up thigh-highs in sheerest Noir. She had to admit the Viennese 70 denier strumpfhose in Pearled Cracked Cement, part of the Urban Disaster collection, tempted her, as well as the Semi-Sheer Velvet Finish Tights in Bruise and Blood Ultra Ultra Red (although any red, and especially a brown-purple red, is particularly unflattering in any-denier sheer, and she decided to wait until they restocked the sold-out opaque version of the tights). But these couldn't match the feel—the promise, really—of the Cashmere Pure-Luxury, woven with the tiniest bit of nylon and Lycra (to make the cashmere cling and not bunch, barely detectable, a soft breath, a whisper on skin). When she spotted the last pair in medium, in the sort of oatmeal cream that would make her feel October and Ivy League, coed and coquettish, or at least like a sort of wrapped Christmas treat, all warm and inviting to touch, she said yes, knowing, in a sinking way, it was obscene. She just wouldn't think about it—not even attempt the usual relativism of what was three hundred dollars here or there: Two couples out for dinner? A plane ticket to Seattle and back? One month's health insurance? An evening's worth of cocaine?— and, actually, not thinking about certain things had become so easy lately, so much a newfound capacity of her conscious will. And by Friday the Winter-Spring Collection, such as Luscious Lent in Satin-Finish Ash, and even Ramadan Rayon Rose, in a more modest 170 denier, would be in, for preview, to the most special and loyal customers. A group with whom Mina surely belonged.

She had large, full thighs. David moved Gwen on the bed, her body the anchor of their afternoons; he could move against it and it would both resist and respond to him. Braque. No, something softer, undulative and layered. Bellini-folded intricacies, a labyrinth of other flesh. It almost upset him, repulsed him, but it did not. So close to disgust it was bracingly erotic, a giving over to all things unlooked at, unexplored. Here was exuberance in flesh. His larger and older lover, Gwen. Long married and with a grown child, Gwen.

Desire transforms you. David believed this.

Leg crooked on his lower back, white, dimples, soap, the soap scent of her thighs. He felt male and small. Hardness overcome by sheer presence, and age, too. Gwen was forty-four. David was thirty. She wasn't at all like the women he had desired his whole life. His whole life.

It wasn't a transformation. It was a conversion.

They whispered affection for parts. I love your hair (curly, silky brown). I love your hands (oddly delicate fingers, unpolished nails). I love your lips (his were not quite full, but evenly balanced, a pout-threatening shapely upper lip). Why, Gwen, do we say I love this and I love that, but we never say I love Gwen, I love David? When do the parts equal the person? But he didn't say this because she didn't want talk, she wanted murmurs and sighs. He didn't ask anything of her because what if she said no? What he feared was a question and an answer that might unhinge their desire. The alchemy of what they were, he wanted desperately to not decompose it, not unravel it, because it felt like random fortune, shakable by temperature and seasons and hormones. He said nothing, held his curiosity back. How odd that it seemed necessary to command such restraint in the execution of a passion. Strange, you fall into an affair because you long to give in to pleasure, to surrender, and then you have to fight yourself to limit the character of your desires. The resistance mixes with the desire, and it becomes something else, some other new thing. It becomes part of the pleasure.

"Mina?"

"Hi, Jack."

"How are you, kiddo?"

"I'm a little late for work."

"Okay."

"How are you?"

"Great. Melissa and I are going to a sweat lodge retreat in Montana for a few weeks. I thought maybe you would want to come."

"Jack, I have responsibilities. A job. I can't just leave. Besides, I don't want to go to a sweat lodge."

"How are things with David?

"Fine. I'll fill you in when I have more time. I'm very late."

"Okay. Mina?"

"What?"

"Michael got released from the hospital. I mean he checked out."

"He did?"

"Yeah. He might contact you. I tried to call him at the hospital, and they said it's been a couple of weeks. He'll try and contact you. If he does, maybe you could go see him. You know, he's—"

"Yeah, I know. He hasn't contacted me. I can't worry about this now. My life is very chaotic. I can't be worried about Michael."

"What's wrong? Is there something you want to talk about?"

"No, it's just the usual sort of insanity. Look, I have to go. I'm sorry."

"I understand. Well, if you hear something, let me know."

"How can I do that if you're on an Indian reservation? Would that be smoke signals?"

"I'll have my mobile phone. I'll be checking my voice mail."

"I haven't heard from him."

Mina had not seen Michael in years. Michael's first episode, leading to his first hospital stay, seemed to come out of nowhere, or to be completely inevitable, depending on how she chose to look at it. Her father had looked to her—you know Michael, tell me what happened. You were always so close. Mina and Michael. Mina had adored Michael.

Then, before all the hospitals, there was the warmth of unbroken companionship. A person so close you hardly needed to speak. The combustible energies and combat closeness of children growing up together, moved around, variously parented. Interior logics developed. Secret reference points. An unquestioned and uncontrived siege bonding.

At seven and ten they spent most of their summertimes apart and with different parents. Michael on location with their father, Mina in L.A. with their mother. But during the school year they were always together. Mina and Michael became a two-person investigative cadre. They experimented, they were on a reconnaissance mission between themselves and the world. She mostly remembered them always lighting things in the fireplace. They would load the kindling and the newspapers and then the Duraflame log and then the real logs in the slate-manteled Beverly Hills fireplace. They would beg to be the one who lit the paper in three or four spaced-out places. The flare-up as it ignited, and then the flare-down as it worked on the wood and the "durable" flame. She liked the initial burning flash, and they were bored with the quietly crackling logs, the stoic heat-giving red glow. If the paper and the twigs burned so brightly, why not do the whole fire with paper and twigs? She had a fantasy of throwing endless paper and twigs as the flames flared and hungrily consumed. The drama of it.

"It doesn't last, doesn't give off heat, it makes too much ash," their father would say. But Michael and Mina would sit as close to the fire as possible, until their faces were red from it, until they couldn't stand it. And when their father wasn't looking, they'd chuck in newspapers, rolled and tied in a knot, so the flames could unknot it, flaring and then waning and sending little flaming pieces up the flue. They would float upward and glow as if in slow motion. And it would look for a moment how they imagined real fires would look, burning houses and cities, when the sky would be filled with pretty glowing bits of slow-rising ash.

Michael took to drawing, on construction paper, skylines and houses. First cityscapes in silhouette, a skyline seen only in movies and nightlife commercials. Mina would cut the edges out, leaving the varied points, the profile of a grand city with six Empire State Buildings, "skyscrapers," jagged, manic-edged buildings built with such upward optimism and hubris they scraped the sky. They'd put it there behind the Duraflame, prop it up before the fire was lit. Then when it started to burn, they would narrate it. They'd become broadcasters. Even break down on the air — "My God, the flames are consuming the city. I've never seen anything like this, my God" — and then they would bawl and scream and cry, finally mimicking the imagined screams of a burning city, even the rats in the boiling sewers.

Their father told them the great Chicago fire started when a cow knocked over a lamp. Mina wondered later why a cow was in the city. And how a fallen lamp could start a fire. Michael figured the smallest mistake could burn the whole world down. One careless moment. They discussed fire drills. Escape plans. Window jumps that could be survived. Mina said, "Well, our house won't burn because it's brick," but he reminded her that whole steel-girdered buildings burn, and brick was even worse. All the fire got locked inside with the people.

"What's a pizza oven made out of, like the one at Mario's?" Mina knew what he was getting at. She nodded sagely.

"Our house is a brick oven."

Then there was the garage. The metal-plated heat toy in the garage. It melted rubber pellets into creatures. It was called Creature Features. Then they discovered Shrinky Dinks, which were plastic, maybe Plexiglas, ornaments that you colored with a special marker and then put in the toaster oven until they shrank and their colors were sealed in, emitting an odd, burning-plastic smell that her brother and she fell in love with. They watched them shrink through the oven window. The melting preset pellets soon inspired their own heat "experiments." They both seemed to realize simultaneously that anything plastic could melt, and that the fun of it, the mystery contained within the plastic, was watching how it would melt. Objects lost their form and revealed something elemental and basic. The truth of things was revealed in their destruction.

Michael's army men succumbed first. They arranged two in static combat on a piece of tinfoil, locked them in the toaster oven, and narrated the results.

"Nuclear combat," Mina said.

"Napalm is covering the hillside," her brother said. The army men would darken, then all at once seem animated and start to buckle and move until they did begin to melt, their guns and arms indistinguishable, drippy appendages, their legs molten with the enemies' legs. They'd stop it midmelt and let them dry, melted together—half men, half mutant blobs.

"They're discovered like this, after the bomb."

"Like Pompeii," she said. Their little Joe faces melted so their entire heads looked like mouths screaming. Soon they had whole postapocalyptic armies, mass graves of melted, screaming men. The kitchen smelled foreign and toxic. Soon anything plastic found its way to the oven, had to be melted. Transformed by heat, watched through the window of the toaster oven. Later it occurred to Mina they were amazingly unsupervised as children. Didn't anyone notice they were melting the entire world, from poker chips to Barbie heads to swizzle sticks? Couldn't people smell it?

"You exaggerate," she had said, years later, to Michael in one of his lucid moments. "One time, one afternoon, we melted an army guy in the toaster. I think the rest is just your pyro fantasies."

But no, she was lying. She remembered. There was fire,

and there was heat. Later there were the days of secret cigarettes on the roof, the red coals the only thing visible as they sat. She wanted to say, You tried to teach me how to do smoke rings, but it was like whistling with two fingers—one of those things you seemed able to do from instinct that I could never learn. But she didn't say that.

The hospital. When she finally forced herself to visit Michael in the hospital, it was her first and last time. He chainsmoked, making an ugly sucking sound until the gesture seemed odd and foreign and creepy. She tried to ignore it, and then she saw under his robe maybe a hundred crescent-shaped, white puckered burns. Circles with the same diameters as cigarettes. Over and over on his skin. Over and over, not once, not a fire and heat experiment, not curiosity or a flirtation with danger—but a mechanical difference. Over and over like the strange sucking sound he made when he inhaled. Mina didn't want to think about that, didn't want to think of him like that. Wouldn't.

But it wasn't really the hospital. The estrangement started long before. The hospital was just the final articulation of it. The first time she noticed how different he was, how he had really changed, was during Thanksgiving vacation his freshman year at college.

Michael had had a rough start at school. He hadn't made any friends. He was on again and off again with Lorene. He hadn't called Mina much at all. Mina missed him completely; his visit was about the only thing she looked forward to that fall. But the strange thing was the longing didn't stop after his return, it was still there as a kind of quiet sadness that couldn't be comforted, sadness about how distant he seemed, sadness about not being ten. He was glamorously lean muscled and suddenly tall. He wore a trench coat and a torn black T-shirt. He carried a dog-eared book, some Latinate-titled philosophy thing, which he fingered at times. He pretended that nothing had changed, jumping her and wrestling, giving her looks at dinner, watching midnight TV and giggling. But he fell into longer, more obscure monologues. He was almost patronizing.

"What do you want to do tonight?" she asked him.

"One—light air. Two—light breeze," he said.

"What?"

"Three—gentle breeze. Four—moderate breeze. Five—fresh breeze. Six—"

"What are you talking about?" She looked up at him. He clutched his book and smiled, as though he was joking.

"Six—strong breeze. Seven—moderate gale. Eight—fresh gale. Nine—strong gale. Just who is she, this Gale? I want to meet this minxish thing."

"Shut up."

"Ten—whole gale. Oh, yes, yes, yes." He laughed and clutched his book. His fingernails were dirty.

"If you don't stop, Michael, I'm going to leave the room."

"Eleven—storm. Twelve through seventeen—hurricane."

"Will you just stop this?" Mina walked to the doorway and glared at him.

"Wait, Mina, wait, the best part, over seventeen—devastation." Michael smiled.

"Why do you do that? I hate when you recite things. It has nothing to do with anything. What's your problem?" Michael just stared at her, for a moment confused, then he laughed.

"I don't know, it's funny." Michael looked at her. "I'm sorry."

"You're weird. You act strange," Mina said, pouting, moving back to the couch. "What's with that book? Is it really necessary to carry it with you at all times?"

"This? I like to read it sometimes." Michael tossed the book in front of her. Mina ignored it. He smiled at her, then spoke flatly. "All propositions are of equal value. The sense of the world must lie outside the world. In the world everything is as it is and happens as it does happen. In it there is no value—and if there were, it would be of no value."

"Michael—"

He continued, smiling as if he were telling a joke, his eyes glancing right as they always did when he recited things, his performance face. Michael had always been what Mina's father called mnemonically performative. But not so relentlessly, not with *her*.

"If there is a value which is of value, it must lie outside all happening and being-so. For all happening and being-so is accidental. What makes it nonaccidental cannot lie in the world, for otherwise this would again be accidental. It must lie outside the world. Hence there are no ethical propositions."

"Yeah, whatever." Mina picked up the remote control and started skipping channels with a ridiculous velocity. "I'm sure you could recite the whole thing and I would never speak to you again. So stop. It's—" She saw he was looking at the book, and she could tell he was saying it anyway, to himself. She felt he was not only not her brother, but a sort of imposter who took the superficial details of Michael and distorted them, ridiculed them.

"So like what's it about, anyway?" she asked. He stopped his trance and looked at her.

"I don't know. Mina, I have no idea. It's abstracting yourself, well, self-reference, anyway, to a kind of philosophical autism. It's like falling off a cliff, and then you're stuck in a labyrinth of solipsism."

"Yeah, whatever. Like as if anything you said actually means anything to me."

"Well, that's the point."

"*What . . .* ever."

He frowned at her. "When did you become so flip?"

"I don't know, maybe when you became such a freak." She shook her head. He stopped fingering the book.

"Look," he said, gesturing at the TV. "*Imitation of Life.*"

"Who cares," Mina said. "I hate those old movies."

"Yeah, right, Mina." Michael smiled and tried to pull her down to the floor next to the TV.

"Don't."

"Mina, Lana Turner. Did you hear me? *Lana. Lana Turner.* Just her name, the way it sounds, like *wanna turn her.* Her aging platinum-poached face. Her turbaned head. Her dressing gown, her vanity set. All those amazing Edith Head clothes." Mina reluctantly glanced at the TV. Michael took her hand and pulled her to the floor in front of Lana's Technicolor fuchsia-lipped head.

"Frosted everything," she said.

"Sandra Dee, Mina," Michael said.

"Troy Donahue."

Mina put the phone down. She had to check in with the restaurant. Then she had to see Max. Again. Nearly every day now. Just the thought of how it would go once she got there, how they would start right in without talking, was enough to make her feel better.

*   *   *

VIDEO #2

Outside MAX'S house. Surveillance black and gray, video hazy. Static angle down on doorway. Obviously from a fixed security camera. We see nothing but the doorway for a moment.

TITLE: ARRIVALS AND DEPARTURES

GIRL appears at door. Her face has been pixelated to obscure her features. She is wearing a sun hat. She leans into the intercom. She pauses for a moment, then pushes the door open.

CUT TO: SAME DOORWAY AGAIN.

Exact same shot of still entrance. The door opens and GIRL exits. She pauses, puts on her sunglasses, and walks off camera.

CUT TO: SAME DOORWAY AGAIN.

GIRL enters the frame, no sunglasses. She pauses, opens her purse, and takes out a compact. She checks her face, touches her hair. She returns compact to purse and presses buzzer. She waits, looks directly at camera, and waves. She rests her hand on the doorknob and then goes inside.

CUT TO: SAME DOORWAY AGAIN.

Entrance is empty for a few seconds. The door opens and
GIRL exits, rushing right off camera in an instant.

CUT TO: SAME DOORWAY AGAIN.

END TITLE: A MINAMAX PRODUCTION

Two Weeks from Leaving

Saturday.

Mina had to go to work today.

Lorene called her early, waking her. She sounded upset,
but Mina pretended not to notice. All she could think about
was no Max today. Instead she would have to cover the lunch
shift at the restaurant. She would have to get it together and
smile and be the face of calm and confidence. She had lied to
David about having to work and now she really did have to
work.

Lisa had to go to work today.

The twins could not be left with their father on Saturdays.
He slept in and by the time he was up and about, the children
had been awake for hours. In his misery and exhaustion, he
had no patience. Mrs. Brenshaw was feeling ill today and
couldn't baby-sit even for a few hours. Lisa decided she would
take the children to Lorene's. She'd let them play in the living
room and watch TV while she cleaned. This was not allowed
by her company. But she couldn't leave them alone with Mark.

Lorene did not have to go to work today.

She canceled her appointments and her session with Beryl at St. John's. She would stay in bed and do nothing. She would let Mina handle everything and sleep in.

She would perhaps spend the day under her sheets, in the dark, trying to be still. She was contemplating some self-touch therapy when she heard the door unlock. She froze under her sheets, and then she remembered Saturday morning the cleaning woman, Lisa, came. She wouldn't have any peace, not even one morning of it. She put on a chartreuse vintage silk kimono painted with tiny Eiffel Towers and black velvet Chinese slippers with sequins. She went down the spiral stairs intending to ask Lisa to cancel today's cleaning. In the living room Lisa had her two five-year-olds, each grasping one hand. They were a boy and a girl, and Lorene watched as the heavy-set woman arranged them on her couch with their toys in front of her large TV. Lisa had on a T-shirt that said "California" in looping cursive letters, with a stylized palm tree punctuating the final *a*.

"Mom, it's much bigger than our TV," the boy said.

"Yes, it is. Now, you guys watch cartoons just like at home. Don't touch anything. Sit right here and afterward we'll get ice cream."

The children nodded and smiled and were already too occupied with the TV to bother with their mother any longer. When Lisa turned away from the kids and saw Lorene, she nearly fell back.

"Lorene. I didn't know you were here."

Lorene waved at her, smiling.

"I'm playing hooky today, Lisa. Are these your children?"

"Yes. I'm sorry. I'll take them home right now. I couldn't get

a sitter, so I brought them. I've never done that before, but I figured it wouldn't be a big deal. I should have checked with you.
I'm so sorry."

Lorene shrugged and looked at the children, mesmerized
by her TV.

"It's all right. They seem like well-behaved kids. What the
hell. What are they, twins?"

"Yes. It's OK? Are you sure?"

Lorene shrugged.

"Yeah, just go ahead and do your work. I'm going to have
some coffee." Lorene sat in her kitchen sipping coffee and
watching Lisa do her routine. It was strange to watch a stranger
clean your house. Lorene felt oddly fascinated. It was embarrassing, really, but in truth she found the company comforting.
It distracted her from herself, and she didn't mind sort of thinking about someone else.

"You do a good job, Lisa. You're very thorough." Lisa
sprayed the oven with oven cleaner, then readied the bucket
and mop for the floor.

"Thank you. Your house is pretty easy. It doesn't seem like
you even live here sometimes."

"I guess you can tell a lot about someone from cleaning
their house."

Lisa scrubbed the countertops. She looked at Lorene in her
silk kimono. Lorene finger-combed her blue-black hair, pushing the ends forward so the curl cut against her cheekbone. An
inward glance at an old photo of Louise Brooks that Lorene
had permanently etched in her brain inspired this early morning primping. Lisa shrugged a shoulder up to her cheek to
move her hair out of her steamy face. When that didn't suffice,
she lifted one wet yellow-glove-clad hand and brushed her hair

back with the peek of forearm where the glove stopped. Still it was in her way.

"I think there are these people who analyze these things—what a person's trash says about them, their dirt, the kind of debris they create. I think it's supposed to be quite telling," Lorene said.

"Yes, I guess so. If you really think about it, but I'm not sure why someone would. Basic things. Whether they have kids or not. What they eat or don't eat. Whether they entertain or not."

"Come on, more than that. What music they listen to, what books they read—or if they read. What clothes they wear, and how much they spend on clothes."

"You have a lot of beautiful clothes."

Lorene nodded.

"So what do you think? I mean, you've cleaned my house for a couple of years now. What conclusions have you drawn?" Lorene hated herself for asking; she turned every situation into an exercise in self-contemplation. Her favorite subject, herself. Lisa looked at her oddly as she continued scrubbing.

"I don't know. Do books and clothes really tell you all that much about a person? I wouldn't know much from that. I think just talking to you now is more about you than all the stuff I clean in your house."

"How so?"

"That you seem more like a person in a movie than any person I've ever met. Everything about you seems so—I don't know. So arranged."

Lorene smiled at this. "Yes, that's true. Rehearsed for some performance."

"And you are aware of this. It kind of pleases you, I can see."

Lorene took out her first cigarette of the day. She caught

Lisa glancing at it, and Lorene made a bit of a show of lighting it.

"Well, isn't maturity about recognizing who you are and running full-throttle toward it?"

"You're not messy."

"It's either maturity or glamour. I haven't figured out which one yet."

"That's a pretty terrible thing to say. Cynical."

"I'm glad to hear I'm not messy," Lorene said. There was a pause and Lisa finished rinsing out the sink. She turned off the water. She looked at Lorene, who stubbed out her cigarette. A million half-finished cigarettes. What do you make of that. Lisa peeled off the gloves.

"Lisa."

Lisa looked over at her again.

"Lisa, by the way, I'm not cynical."

"I'm sorry, it's just, you . . ." Lisa glanced around the room and then looked directly at Lorene. "You have a lot of beautiful things. You have a peaceful, safe place to be. I don't feel sorry for you."

Lorene almost laughed. Women like Lisa used to really admire her. It was a given, an absolute certainty. What had happened?

"You're sort of a smart cookie, huh? Fair enough. I asked, after all. And when I talk to you, I don't ask you any questions about your life, do I?"

Lisa smiled at her, shrugging.

"I noticed that, too."

"So what occupies you, if not some performance of yourself?"

"What occupies me? My family. My family, my family and, oh, yeah, my family."

"Your kids?"

"That's what I said, my family."

"And their father?"

Lisa shrugged again.

"Their father is an unwilling participant." She put the cleanser in the cupboard and shut it. "I have to clean your bedroom now."

Lorene nodded over her coffee. "I'm sorry. Go ahead."

Lorene could hear Lisa getting the vacuum cleaner from the hall closet and carrying it slowly up the stairs. Soon afterward she heard the sound of the vacuum running in the bedroom. Something almost crossed her mind about what it would be like to be Lisa instead of herself. Almost. She crossed her legs and her kimono opened loosely, revealing one white smooth knee and one hairless creamy thigh. She examined her leg, pushing her hand across her smooth skin, sitting alone in her pristine kitchen.

Mina walked the two miles to Vanity and Vexation. She had to break her date with Max, stop in and check on the other two restaurants, then return to V and V for a meeting with the designer, then make it home in time for dinner with David. She hadn't read the postcard in her pocket. She knew it was another one from Michael. When she arrived at the Gentleman's Club, she had phone messages to call her father, her mother, and Lorene. She ignored these. Then she received a phone call.

"Mina?"

"Yes?"

"It's Scott."

"Yes."

"You don't seem too happy to talk to me."

"Well, I'm busy."

"I'm in town."

"But you were just here."

"I know, but I need to talk to you."

"I just saw you."

"I have to see you."

"I'm really busy. "

"But I really have to see you."

"OK, OK. Not today, though. Sunday. Three o'clock."

Mina walked back along Wilshire to Food Baroque.

When you ignore me, I feel as if I don't exist.

The card was of two Indians holding corn. She folded it and put it away. She had to get to the restaurant and supervise the new reservationist. Allison, or maybe Alysyn. No, it was Ashley. Or Ashleigh.

Mina had followed Michael to her parents' bedroom. Thanksgiving vacation, Michael's first visit home from college. But it was "Michael," now college-distanced, Michael 2.0, the latest version, the imposter. He took her hand and said he wanted to show her something. A secret. He actually looked over his shoulder stealthily. It felt for a moment as if they were not teenagers on the verge of dreaded adulthood, but kids again, on a covert, invented mission. She felt a momentary sort of relief. He went to their father's antique rolltop desk and pulled out one of the drawers. He reached to the back of the drawer and pulled out a hand-sized box. It was inlaid wood with different-colored stain and a smooth satin finish with rounded edges. One of those horrible Santa Barbara craft shop boxes tourists buy, with secret smooth, airtight compartments obviously built for drug stashing. Michael slid open the main compartment. Inside were several small screw-top glass vials full of white powder, and a folded Ziploc bag full of empty gelatin capsules. Mina couldn't hold back an audible gasp, which made Michael cover her mouth with his hand.

"Shut up," he whispered. He opened one vial and sniffed at the opening. He inserted a pinkie in the top and tasted the powder. He had seen this in cop shows a million times, he was well prepared.

"I think that's your everyday cocaine," and he made a stage-yawn gesture. He reached for the next vial and repeated the cop-show bit.

"That looks grayer and clumpier," Mina whispered.

"Well, it's not cocaine," he whispered, and made a face indicating a bitter flavor. "I wonder what drug it could be? Maybe I should ask Daddy."

"Put it away and let's get out of here," she whispered, looking at the doorway. "What difference does it make what it is?"

"One way to find out," Michael said. Looking at him, she realized he was enjoying this discovery quite a lot. Then, in a gesture of huge import, something Mina would never forget, a point of difference that would be turned over and over and referred to for years to come, her brother looked straight at her, leaned back his head, put the vial to his mouth, and tapped the entire contents into the back of his throat. He swallowed hard a couple of times. Amazing, exceptional Michael. He had the giddy, exalted air of someone who had just proved something dramatic to himself, even if it wasn't clear yet what that was, or maybe the giddiness came from not knowing the precise consequences and just waiting for the fallout. Mina thought again about the newly surfaced difference between them, beyond age or gender or geography, but a categorical difference, an absolute, italic difference.

"Are you, like, fucking nuts?" She felt tiny and frightened.

"Shh, it's OK. Jut get me some water."

A half hour later it was time for the family meal. They sat at the dining room table, the entire family and the friends who were included as family. Lately—actually, *precisely*—since her incident with Dennis, her father's best friend, she regarded these friends as intrusive, creepy, envious types. Sort of Anne Baxter-ish groupie characters, admiring her family but deeply resenting it, too. Right next to her father sat Dennis, as if everything were the same—he had said to forget it ever happened, and, look, he had. And her father's assistant, Sheila. Smiling at her. All these familiar people now had shadow selves to Mina, as she did herself. But these were only minor distractions compared with Michael. She didn't take her eyes off him once as they began eating. Michael seemed unaffected. He ate and conversed and even quoted a whole monologue from a movie, flashing his dazzling golden-boy smile.

"Say, Mike, what are you studying out there?" Dennis asked him. Michael looked at him and took a sip of water.

"Michael is going to take a graduate philosophy course next semester," Jack said.

"As a freshman?"

"He got to skip his required undergraduate philosophy survey."

Mina pushed the food around on her plate, estranged from her own body, abstracting eating into a hideous, complicated thing. Her family invaded by pod people, or what was that movie? Where they all look familiar but they have really been stolen away? They all seemed to be having so much fun, Michael included. Mina felt as if she had taken the mystery vial of white powder, that she must be the one invaded by foreign entities.

Now Michael started to eat very slowly.

"Where do you think you'll go to graduate school?" Sheila asked. Michael stared at his fork as if it had suddenly become an object of mysterious function.

"Are you going to go to film school?" Dennis said. They all looked at Michael, who was cautiously pressing the tines of the fork into a baby carrot. He glanced up at the adults looking expectantly at him. There was an awkward pause.

"There's this place in New Mexico."

"A film school?" Jack said skeptically.

Michael grasped his fork tightly and stared at his fist.

"It's this valley. And this guy put these stainless-steel rods, four hundred of them, equidistant, precise, in a field out in this valley." Michael gave up on the fork and started to smile but still didn't look up. Jack sort of laughed uneasily.

"So the delineated space, this grid, is exactly a mile long and a kilometer wide. Four hundred rods out there to attract lightning. Just for its own sake. That's the idea, anyway." Michael stopped smiling. "And it's there, right now, this very moment, these hundreds of precisely aligned, perfectly spaced lightning rods in a field in a valley about two hundred miles south of Albuquerque, New Mexico." There was a pause as everyone nodded at Michael and then went back to eating. Jack asked if anyone wanted more wine, and conversation resumed in a different direction and Mina continued to watch Michael, waiting for him to say something to her or glance her way.

He wore a look of extreme concentration. He gamely grasped the fork once again, lifting it with a mechanical deliberateness, then closed his mouth on it, following with a labored and protracted swallow. Slowly the fork went down again to the plate, and then the long way back to his mouth. Eating had become too conscious for him to accomplish, although he seemed determined to continue. She again tried to catch his eye. Later we will both laugh about this, right? He continued to eat even more slowly. He finally dropped the fork and stood up. He excused himself and left the room. Not a glance or a wink or an eye roll in her direction. No one seemed to give much notice to his abrupt exit. They accepted it as standard moody teenaged behavior. They shrugged and commented faintly about Michael "doing his own thing" and "letting him work it out."

Mina heard the revving of his Alfa Romeo. Michael peeled out of the driveway, leaving her with the pod people, all alone.

Hours later, he woke her with a tap on the arm. She had fallen asleep still in her clothes, on top of the bedspread, lights on. Michael was sitting on her bed.

"Jesus, are you OK?" she said.

"No, I'm Michael," he said, giggling.

"You're, you're like so fucking crazy, Michael."

He looked a little wild-eyed but recovered; in fact, he glowed with an aloof, distracted sort of amusement.

"I thought you were like splayed across Sunset Boulevard."

"Like, like, like yeah?" he said, giggling some more.

"What?" Mina asked, rubbing her eyes.

"Am I, like, crazy? No, I'm, like, OK, a nearly perfect facsimile of OK but not actually OK. But *like* OK."

"Stop it."

"*Like* stop it, or really stop it?"

"Fuck, Michael."

"I've been thinking, Mina, that a person could speak only using the words *like, yeah, yah,* and perhaps *as if* and communicate purely by inflection and gesture. You know, like," and he nodded and then he shrugged.

"Stop it."

"It's Zen language, minimal, pure, all reduced to context and intonation. Hyperbolic emphasis. All complications of meaning reduced to these porous words, as meaningful or as meaningless as you choose. Erasing language, pure inflection. Pure speech. So nonspecific it encompasses everything, sort of, like, profound, you know? We could call it "like" speaking."

"Are you OK?"

"Like, yeah." Michael raised the inflection on the last part of *yeah* as if to say, That is obvious. *So* obvious.

"I screwed up, Mina," Ashlee said. She was twenty-two and astoundingly tan.

"What do you mean?" Mina flicked on the reservation computer.

"I mean I entered the wrong information for Mrs. Bradley last night."

"Is that a real tan? Or is that one of those self-bronzers?"

"I entered someone else's information, and it was supposed to be no fish, but we used a fish stock, and she's allergic to —"

"Mrs. Bradley? You mean Dale Bradley's second wife? You don't mean that Mrs. Bradley, do you?"

"She called. She had to go to the hospital. Mr. Bradley wants to talk to you. He's in the lounge downstairs. The Room."

Mina smiled grimly and looked at the video monitor of the lounge. Mr. Bradley.

"It's a real tan. I mean, I got it at a tanning salon."

"Ashlee, tell him I'm not here. Or, wait. No, here's what you do. You go downstairs to Mr. Bradley. You tell him you screwed up and you start to cry. Maybe you even lean on him a little because you are so upset. You tell him you screwed up and you beg him not to tell me because I'll fire you and you really, really need this job. Think, I don't know, think of Sharon Tate in *Valley of the Dolls*—beautiful and helpless."

Ashlee nodded.

"And Ashlee—use your tan. That's very bold, a real tan. Very bold."

"But Mina?"

"What?"

Ashlee looked very upset.

"What?"

"I don't know who Sharon Tate is."

Mina smiled. "That's perfect, Ashlee. Perfect, spot-on. Now go down there."

The phone buzzed.

"It's me."

"Hi." Mina watched Ashlee on the video monitor. She looked great. Extremely tan.

"Mina."

"I can't come over this afternoon."

"Yeah, I know."

"I think I'm going crazy."

"Tomorrow. Sunday."

"Uh, Christ, I can't. I have to meet with Lorene—not possible."

"Are you wearing a skirt? Or are you wearing pants?"

"No."

"Just tell me and I'll let you go. Are you alone?"

"I'm watching Ashlee kiss a customer on the video monitor. Ashlee with two *e*'s and no *y*, Max."

There was a long Max silence.

"Max?"

More silence. Mina sighed. "How about tomorrow noon?"

"Yep."

Mr. Bradley had his arm around Ashlee. His hand moved to her tiny waist. Her body was shaking with sobs. Max hung up the phone and Mina waited for the dial tone. Max wasn't able to disconnect and she listened to the repeated clicks as he pressed the cradle button again and again to hang up. At last, she heard the dial tone.

Lorene sat at her kitchen table, still in her kimono at noon. She kept staring at the mail she had from yesterday. A white envelope with no return address and familiar handwriting was tucked among bills and magazines. It was Michael's handwriting. Inside was a card with a picture of the Chrysler Building. It read: *Left the hospital and am going to visit Mom in New York. Be there until end September. I'll be in touch. I'm sorry it's been so long. I hope you are all right.*

She did some calculations strung together by weather systems, riots, disasters, and shoe styles. It was three years since he'd contacted her. Nothing since the one time she saw him in the hospital. The *one* time he had reluctantly agreed to let her visit him.

She had found him surrounded by papers—tacked to the wall, in stacks on the floor. He had been busy compiling lists, it seemed. For unknown purposes.

Lorene wore a pale peach crepe de chine day dress that had been altered with strips of peek-a-boo peach lace inserted at bias-cut angles. Underneath she wore a deep auburn silk sheath slip, and under the slip, nothing at all, save some very sheer flesh-colored stockings that stopped midthigh. The stockings were held in place by embroidered garters, tiny peach flowers on beige, the elastic kind of garter that just circled each thigh around the top band of the stocking. It was all, she realized as she entered the room, far too precious, far too much. She cringed in the doorway — a mistake. Couldn't she have just been simple and sober for once? He sat on a single tightly and grayly made-up institutional bed, looking thin and tender in a fresh white T-shirt and drawstring pants. He had the air of incarceration. He was engrossed in the papers he held, and it took him a full minute to notice her standing in the doorway. He stared at her, took her in, and she wished with all her heart she had worn underwear.

He smiled. "Is this a dream?" he said. His voice was deeper than she remembered. This comforted her in a way.

"Hi, Michael," she said. He sat, so thin that it seemed as he leaned forward that his arms might buckle, and then, of course, there was Michael's face. Having not seen him for so long, she could no longer visualize his face. Her memory of it was Cubist, thought of in pieces. She remembered his nose and his dark eyes. His mouth too, but the sum was beyond her. And now here he was, the present apparition, and she looked at him quickly before she had to look away. It was always painful to look at someone she hadn't seen in a while, the way time is inescapably written on a face. She looked again. It was Michael, yes, but, God, oh, God. He was much more angular, of course. It jarred her. Only a couple of years (actually four) had passed since she'd last seen him, yet she still remembered him as perpetually seventeen, the summer she first met him. No one was younger than Michael at seventeen, no one had more grace in his animation. His confident glide through the world writ all over his smooth cheeks and in his large eyes. He was, at twenty-six, no longer young. His hair was cropped very short, chopped, actually, tight against his head. His new angles made his dark eyes larger than ever, and there was tension in his mouth. His lips were thinner and straighter. He was still handsome, but in a dusty, sad, desperate way that only men can wear as handsome, so distant from "cute," so far from the young man she remembered.

"You are still my most beautiful Lorene," he said, slightly too loud, and he smiled again. His teeth were bigger than she remembered, but recognizable, not that far off, almost OK. She knew she should approach him, hug him or touch him. But she just stood. She took off her sunglasses.

In addition to the bed, the room had a wood chair and a desk. The chair faced the bed. There was a computer on top of the desk, and a small window above the computer. The opposite wall was stacked with books. The afternoon light from the window was the only illumination, but even in its dust-filled haziness, it was stark enough, and she found her way to the chair, sat, crossed her legs at the ankles and tucked them under the chair. He leaned in toward her from the bed, elbows on knees, and lit a cigarette. He did not stop looking at her, or smiling at her. After a minute, he stopped smiling and pushed his papers aside. He looked at the room, and back at her, and put the sheet he was writing on facedown on a stack on the floor.

"I'm so tired, Lorene. All the time."

"Me, too," she said, pulling her own cigarettes out of her purse. He reached for his matches and leaned forward to light her cigarette. She put her hand on his match-holding hand — it was shaking. She steadied it as she inhaled. The touch, instantly over, shocked her. She was suddenly ready to cry.

"You gave me this purse," she said. He looked at the black leather square-framed bag she was holding.

"A vintage knockoff of the Hermès bag that was designed for Grace Kelly," she said. He smiled, staring at it.

"Don't you remember?"

"Yes. A knockoff." He looked at her. "Same old Lorene. You're sweet to carry it today."

"I use it a lot. I love my Kelly bag," she said. She emphasized the word love too much, she heard emotion in her own voice, and the sound of it upset her. She was starting to cry, and she had to try not to.

"I'm so glad you came. I'm sorry I couldn't see you sooner. I've had a very tough—"

"I know," she said, stopping him. "I know." She smoked, and looked at her cigarette and felt him watching her, and felt herself falling again, miraculously, into deeply wanting him. So many times she longed to feel these long-remembered feelings, and now it was frightening, wanting him again. But she did. They sat smoking for what seemed like hours, but it wasn't even the duration of one cigarette. He put his out and moved up from the bed. He went to the door and turned the lock.

"They let you—" and she stopped.

"Yeah, I'm allowed to lock my door. They have a key, of course, but I do get to lock the door. It's funny; one is supposed to recover from irrational paranoia in a place of limitless intrusion. Maybe it's to give you a sane context—he's not crazy if we supply a reason for his paranoia by keeping him under constant surveillance," Michael said, laughing. He stood by the door, then took a few steps toward her. She sat frozen, not looking at him.

"It's OK to laugh about it, Lorene," he said.

"But, God, no—" she said, and looked at him.

"What?"

"I'm confused," she said.

"Yeah, you're telling me," and he laughed again. She laughed and then resumed crying.

"I've made you cry already," he said. He stood in front of her and then knelt on the floor by her legs. He put his hand behind one of her feet and started to remove her shoe. He placed it to one side, and then he gently removed the other, placing it neatly by the first one. She put her hand on his head and softly rubbed his hair. He closed his eyes at her touch and then rested his head on her peach crepe-covered knee. He had one hand on her ankle, and as he rested his head against her, he held her ankle lightly with his circled fingers. She stroked his hair, and his ear, and felt a minute release of a subaudible sigh. A body sigh. She was unsure if it was Michael's sigh or her own. She opened her legs a little. Michael lifted his head and stared up at her. Lorene looked at him, slowly pulling her skirt up, over the tops of her knees. He knelt between her thighs, still encir-cling her ankle with his hand. He looked at her legs and slid his hand up from her ankle, moving both hands now slowly along her thighs until his thumbs rested on the bare flesh above her stockings. She sat very still. He closed his eyes, and she felt the tiny touch of his thumbs on her skin. He inched forward and she edged toward him on the hard wood chair until her hips were at his waist and their faces were inches from each other. He lifted his hands and put them on either side of her face, holding her for a moment. It was all so slow and silent. She wanted to kiss him, but she waited until he leaned close and kissed her. It wasn't what she expected, a tentative, initiating kiss, but a deep, hard kiss, a sudden long, intimate kiss, and she opened her mouth as he pressed into her. He tasted metallic, foreign. Then the foreignness faded away. She closed her eyes and felt the room slip away in this opened-mouth intimacy. They were somewhere else, some world of bodies and touch, of thought-effacing pleasure. She only had one conscious thought, lasting a second—when he moved his hand from her face to under her skirt and between her legs—just that thank God she was completely wet and longing for him, and then the thought was gone. His mouth was hungry and unrelenting, but his hand was gentle and coaxing, and when he stopped kissing her and got up, pulling her to her feet and over to his bed, she stopped him and stood apart from him for a moment. She looked at him as she unzipped her dress. He stood by the bed, watching her. She pulled the slip off, over her head, losing sight of him for a moment, but still feeling his gaze on her belly and breasts as she made herself naked. He stood waiting as she bent and removed each stocking. Her gestures weren't slow or urgent, just plain and necessary. When she finished she approached him and lifted his T-shirt. He undid his drawstring pants and sat on the bed pulling them off until he too was naked. She felt suddenly fearful as he put his hands on her waist and then moved them up to the sides of her breasts.

"Michael," she said, pulling back, embarrassed. Her breasts were bigger than the last time he saw her, an unremovable costume, surgically altered in the now old-fashioned way, with tiny visible scars under each. She leaned back from him, tearing again, ashamed.

"Lorene, scars don't scare me," he said, and that must have been true because he had many, many tiny crescent scars on his arms and chest. He reached for her again, and leaned to kiss her nipples and her tiny belly. She was then back, falling under his touch, and kissing his body. Their touching became more urgent and heated. She was finding familiar places in his body—the way his shoulders felt, the muscles in his arm as he stroked her between her thighs. He had not forgotten how she was to be got at, gently but firmly and steadily, sideways almost, until she felt her body reach an almost impossible edge, and he slowed his touch even more, elongating the moment until she felt a sheet of horizontal pleasure slide out to the farthest points of her body and then resolve in a deep shudder. She lingered in it, shaking through her climax, and he kept pressing her gently, even more minutely, more tiny-ly until from somewhere far off another wave of shudders came, until she was crying from it. Her tears flowed and he kissed her longer and harder.

After they had stopped, as they lay entwined, she still cried softly.

"It's OK, Lori," he said, and he let her cry on his chest. She didn't resist, and she couldn't stop, it was a long-coming release.

"I remember when I used to be able to make you laugh," he said. She started to smile then, but still she was crying.

"You do make me laugh. I remember that, too."

"Lorene—" he said, and she took some breaths and calmed down.

"Lorene."

"What, Michael?" and she looked up at him, his face in profile. He just closed his eyes, smiling slightly, shaking his head.

"What, what are you going to tell me now? That you're crazy? That you can't function? That your obsessions overwhelm reality, that you can't bear the world, or me, or anything but your own four walls in this hospital?"

He opened his eyes and turned his face toward her.

"Uh, no. I was going to tell you that my arm is falling asleep and it's going to go numb if I don't move it out from under where you are resting your head and shoulders. Not right away, mind you, but soon." She laughed and lifted her head from his chest and looked at him.

"See, I've got you laughing now."

"Yeah."

He closed his eyes again, back on the pillow.

"It's very good right now, but it's not always so easy."

She closed her eyes to listen to him.

"Right now, yes, is great. But I have so much trouble."

"What do they say is wrong?"

"I am . . . I find comfort in small, orderly, controllable things."

"Do they give it a name?"

"There is an anxiety that overwhelms me, and concentration is the only—" Michael stopped and shook his head.

"What do your doctors say it is?"

"C'mon, Lorene. What do you want to hear—Neotraumatic Stress Disorder. Nonspecific Anxiety Dysthymia. Bilateral Well-Being Deficiency Disorder. Pseudoautistic Hypermimetic Compulsion. Disassociative Dystopia Anticipation Paranoia." Michael looked at the wall and drummed his fingers. He nearly smiled as he spoke. "Malicious Malingering Syndrome." He glanced at Lorene, then looked away.

"Metallic, endless, vacant thoughts drained of everything but static—" Michael stopped abruptly and stared at his hand.

Lorene opened her eyes and looked at the stacks of papers in the room.

"But here, in this protected place, even with me here, in this place, you're OK."

"It's fleeting. I can already feel things edging in. And this is on a really good day."

"You don't feel good?" she asked.

"It will take me weeks to recover. I can't do this with you."

"But we already did."

"We can't do this again. You have to understand, Lorene."
He was no longer looking at her, but staring at his hand. His
fingers drummed the wall. Lorene sat up, leaned against the
wall. She wanted to edge into his sight.

"You have no faith in me. I am strong, I can handle anything. I can take it."

He smiled, and then he looked away from the wall and
looked at her directly. He shook his head.

"You're always looking for the grand sacrifice, the salvation,
the thing to give yourself over to. But I'm not built for these
things. It's me. I've lost faith in the world as a place I can reli-
ably inhabit. It takes so much energy—so many possible interpretations. No way to distinguish one from the other. A
paralysis, an ambivalence ensues. You're perfect. You have such
overwhelming certainty and confidence. But me? I just can't."

"Can I stay a bit longer?"

"I like small, orderly things I can contain. That I can hold
completely in my head, with an order and an end."

He was driving with one hand on the steering wheel and the
other holding his coffee. She offered to hold his cup for him,
but he waved her off. The kids lay low in the narrow backseat
of the truck. Lisa hated it, it wasn't safe for kids their age, but
they had no choice. Mark kept spilling coffee on his thick fingers, and then when he took a sip of the hot liquid, some of it
spilled on his shirt.

"Goddamn too much to expect a peaceful cup of coffee on
a Sunday morning." He rolled down his window and tossed out

the rest of the coffee. Then he tossed the cup in the foot well on Lisa's side, where she watched it roll out of sight and clink next to two other cups already under the seat.

Lisa went over her shopping list.

"You know I only got thirty hours last week."

She nodded and looked at him. He still had one hand on the steering wheel. The other hand put a cigarette in his mouth and snapped his lighter open, lighting it. He squinted at the dash, half from the noon-bright sun they now faced, and half from the smoke that curled out of his mouth. Lisa opened her window. Glanced at the cigarette and then in the backseat at the kids. She didn't say anything. She didn't have to. She found most things Mark did were bad for the kids to see or hear or have any proximity to. He had learned this by now. She went back to her list, whittling it down to its bare minimum.

"We can't get much. We are already late on rent and the phone and the electric bill will come Monday," he said.

"I've got nine hours' cleaning money coming." He didn't look at her.

"Oh, well, that's a relief. Let's see, that's what? A hundred and ten bucks? And then you gotta give Brenshaw some money to baby-sit, and that leaves about fifty bucks. No, Lisa."

"Mrs. Brenshaw doesn't care if I pay her anything. I just do some shopping for her and go to the post office. I help her cook. That's all."

Mark looked at her and then tossed his cigarette. He put a hand on her plump knee. She had gotten very heavy since the twins, and she'd taken to baggy sweatshirts and jeans. Her hair was pulled back, and she seldom wore lipstick or even earrings. Still, she was smooth-cheeked and young. He held her knee for a moment.

"You need to ask your mother for some help."

Lisa stared out the window.

"No. I can't do that, Mark."

He pulled his hand off her knee and turned the steering wheel leftward, moving the truck into a parking space.

"Don't be this way. We don't have enough money. We are falling way behind."

"Look, I'm not asking her for money. We already owe her money. I'll pick up more cleaning hours. We'll manage."

"No, Lisa, you already can't even manage to keep our apartment clean. There are piles of laundry and there is never any food in the fridge. I'm sick of it. Just ask her for five hundred. It means nothing to her." But it was no use. She was being a stubborn bitch. She was in a foul mood. When she was trying to get him up this morning, he grabbed her arm and told her to give him a break. He just pulled her a tiny bit too hard. He honestly hadn't meant to, and now she would be quiet and angry all day. The kids were quiet in the back, somehow taking Lisa's mood and multiplying it.

Alex gripped his mother's hand as they walked across the parking lot following Mark and Alisa. Alisa did not want to hold her father's hand. She kept pulling back to her mother. He moved too fast across the parking lot. Alisa went limp, a passive resister, her little body made dead weight. When he pulled at her she became a rag doll on the ground. He cursed, shot Lisa a look, then picked Alisa up. She continued to play dead, her head lolling around and her arms limp. She would do this to him. In the living room at bedtime, he'd grab her fast and she'd fall backward, like she'd been dealt a blow. It was kind of disturbing, her dead falls, even from the tiny height of a five-year-old body. She was fearless in her resistance of him. He would continue to pull her, and she would drag on the ground, her legs catching on table legs and doorjambs, until he gave up and picked her up. Then she became suddenly animated, her whole body a writhing, squirming thing, wriggling against his grip. He would nearly drop her, she became so difficult to hold, and he gave up, the five-year-old body outsmarting his huge person.

In the parking lot she did not squirm but continued to play dead. He thought people walking by would think she'd passed out, but at least she wasn't squirming.

Lisa watched the back of Mark and her tiny daughter's head bobbing. Her little face was blank. She wished Alisa wouldn't behave like this toward Mark, but kids were not diplomatic in that way. They were Richter scales of disturbances, tiny, finely calibrated indicators of subarticulated resentments. At the entrance to the Safeway, Mark turned to Lisa and handed her the body of Alisa. Alisa immediately revived and hugged her mother with arms and legs, an exaggerated affection. Alex clung tighter to not just Lisa's hand but her whole forearm. Mark regarded them for a moment, the three of them like refugees in some news footage, huddled under the shellfire of the enemy. He, of course, was the enemy, or the whole world was. Things had become stuck this way. He wanted to appeal to Alex, at least, but instead he turned away from them and strode through the automatic doors, the AC feeling good and momentarily relieving his frustration. He waited by a shopping cart as Lisa walked in, child-upholstered, staggering a bit. She peeled Alisa from her neck and pushed her into the kiddie seat of the shopping cart. Alisa still tried to cling to her from her seat, but Lisa firmly placed her daughter's hands on the cart handle. Mark had his arms folded, watching. Lisa lifted the tight-gripped Alex and placed him standing in the cart next to where his sister sat.

"Are we ready or what?" Mark said, scowling at his watch. Lisa pushed the cart after him, pulling her list out. He led them, although he had nothing specific in mind. She had the list. She stopped behind him, filling the cart with paper towels and jars of peanut butter and tubes of toothpaste. She read labels intently. She studied them. She examined produce. Smelled it. Looked at expiration dates and asked the produce clerk the origins of things. She picked expensive organic chicken. Mark didn't say anything. Time and money were no object to Lisa.

Alex reached for a package of cookies, and Mark grabbed it out of his hands.

"No extras today. We can't afford it." Alex looked at his mother.

"Don't look at her. I'm the walking wallet. Daddy pays, not Mommy."

Lisa pushed the cart forward. Mark shook his head. How did he get to be the one who always said no? She was the one who had too much pride to ask for help.

After the checkout girl took Mark's money, he let Lisa push the cart of packages to the truck. He leaned against the car smoking as she unloaded the bags into the back.

"That's nearly my whole check, Lisa. I have to have some money for gas. And I need some money to go out and blow off some steam tonight. My one night of the week. I have to drink cheap beer and stay home watching TV, is that it? I have to work at five in the morning and I can't even buy a damn hamburger?"

Lisa put the kids in the backseat. They were quiet and pliant, thankfully. He watched her. They were a whole thing, united against him. He stood apart, unregarded. She moved heavily in the front seat and waited for him. He stood in the parking lot; the hot asphalt and the relentless summer California sun made him squint and sweat. He finally got in. She looked at his thick fingers on the steering wheel. It wasn't going anyplace. Things were stuck. They were stuck.

"I'll take care of the rent. I told you," she said.

Mark shook his head.

"But I'm not asking her."

Lisa felt a tiny soft hand on her cheek from the backseat. Her son, Alex, stroked the side of her face that was turned to the car window. A gentle little-boy touch. She reached behind her for his hand.

Spirit Gyms and Miracle Miles

Mina was trying to walk fast from her meeting with Lorene, which naturally she had been late for. First Lorene, then Max, then Scott. She had made Lorene late for an afternoon session at her spirit gym, again, Mina's fault, again. But Mina couldn't help it. She had, in a mere matter of weeks, hopelessly complicated her life. Now it seemed out of her control, a momentum of disaster. And on a Sunday. She remembered, with odd nostalgia, the way Sundays used to be. David and Mina's unassailable day at home. It had all started on a Sunday, though, hadn't it? She had sat on the porch with them, David and Max. An ordinary Sunday afternoon. They sat, drinking beer and eating potato chips, sucking on the occasional hot-weather cigarette. She kept lighting one and then putting it out—it never tasted as good as she imagined, but she kept trying, thinking some subtle chemical change had occurred since the last attempted drag that would make the cigarette as satisfying as she hoped.

If a person—Mina herself, for example—if she were a stranger, passing this porch and taking in this tableaux, here is what she would think: she would envy the handsome group of friends, leisure-wilted, good-looking, laughing and slightly drunk in the afternoon. And the average-looking girl, in the casual company of men and their jokes and their ease. The luck of the girl, with the attention of the two men, and their laughter. What must her life be like? And Mina would see her as if she were in a print ad or a TV commercial, laughing open-mouthed, throwing her head back, shooting pool in a sequined dress, leaning into a sail on a perfect blue sea, throwing an arm up in the swing of a convertible, waving—open-mouthed and impossibly carefree—at unseen friends, but always outnumbered and accompanied by men. Always backlit by their charmed and undivided attentions. What a lucky girl, what a life she has, she would imagine, watching herself. And she's not even beautiful.

David's best friend, Max, sat on their porch steps, unshaven and sweaty, smoking and drinking at twice the pace of the other two. He kept holding the sweating beer bottle to his forehead and rolling it horizontally, occasionally pressing the wet glass to one of his cheeks. David's cheeks looked cool and dry. He wore an Australian army cap with a brim that suited his face, made him cinematic and casually glamorous. Where Max had an apparent early-thirties thin-guy gut that pressed against his T-shirt when he sat hunched, David was sleek, and inoffensively so, no hard-earned ripples in his stomach, just a natural slim elegance that made Mina think, He really isn't like me, is he? It was in a silent pause in the afternoon sun, as she compared Max and David, that it happened. Max looked at her, looked when David wasn't looking, looked when she was looking. He stared at her, and she felt it. It was like that, nearly conscious, although it wasn't, she just made it so when she recalled it, finding reasons and ironies and logic and psychologies. But there, with the heat and the sweating beer bottles and the porch, within exhale reach of David's obscene elegance, Mina nearly fainted with desire for his best friend, Max, his sweat and his soft, decadent body, his chain-smoking, his sideways cynicism, and his dead-on gaze.

She walked faster. Faster and faster. She didn't even notice that above Gower as it crossed Sunset the slightly sloping Hollywood sign was visible through the afternoon haze. From Gower you could see a red-tile-and-adobe church with a tower and a cross atop the tower. And only from this particular vantage point of Gower and Sunset did the cross seem to punctuate the "Hollywood." She didn't notice this today, although it was just the sort of thing she liked to notice, some hyper-unsubtle Babylon irony, one that you could imagine a fifties soundtrack punctuating grandly with telltale-sudden-realization music. One that surely was in some film, at some time.

Lorene watched water collect in pools on the white tile floor.

"Keep breathing," he said. The water moved from rivulets to tiny pools. Eventually, a puddle. It collected, swelling, and then married other nearby puddles. The room must have a drain.

"Concentrate on your breathing only," he said.

She was naked, perched on a bench with her back to him. She felt his hands—large, soft—on her lower back.

"Expand your diaphragm. Expel all your breath slowly."

Mina walked from Max's apartment off Rossmore to Beverly Boulevard. There she turned right and walked to La Brea. She moved briskly, attaining a sort of rhythm she found relaxing, even liberating. She was damp from the shower, and the hot, flat heat of the afternoon streets slowly penetrated her skin, replacing outward dampness incrementally with her own perspiration. She wore no stockings, just bare legs under a cotton dress and flat shoes. She felt peasantish and pure, but with a sort of sexy Sicilian-widow world-weariness. She walked along La Brea down to Wilshire. She walked, quickly as she could, west on Wilshire toward the streamlined moderne facade of the former May Company Department Store dimly visible in the hazy distance. This was it, the Miracle Mile. The first shopping district built for car shoppers instead of pedestrians. She was in true enemy territory now. She walked defiantly on, window-shopping the cul-de-sacs of parking lots, strip mall-ettes, and monolithic gray-faced buildings set back, way back, from the street. There was, miraculously, still a sidewalk. She laughed at this, their lack of commitment. Total car culture shouldn't have sidewalks, should it?

Lorene's Talk-n-Touch Advanced Well-Being Therapy sessions with Beryl were even rougher than basic touch therapy. She sat naked on a towel-covered bench in a steam-filled room. At some point she would have to speak, not incessant rantings, but speak out of some inner hypnotic state. Beryl would lightly touch pressure points on her back, his hands hovering over energy points. Where energy collected, tension would be excised through speech. She felt dizzy. When she took deep breaths, she felt her breasts rise. She was steamy wet; her nipples felt hard and swollen. She looked down with a careful pride. Still perfect, beautiful breasts at thirty-two. Not her original breasts, of course, but from this angle the scars from her breast augmentation were invisible, she had a flawless, natural-looking C cup. They looked even larger, though, because she was so slender and the skin was so white. She thought, I want the whole world to see my breasts. She almost laughed at the absurdity of this, but it was halfway true. Here was the greatest cultural asset a girl could have (attained at no small expense) and no one had seen them in years.

"You can begin speaking at any time, Lorene. Just speak without editing. Just let the words flow out of you." Christ. She closed her eyes. His hands were on her lower back. They felt good. She wouldn't mind showing Beryl her breasts. Forget Beryl, call the old man himself, St. John. He could put his hands on her breasts. If the warm, large healer hands moved from back to front, if they started to rub and pull at her nipples very gently—Lorene felt the dampness between her legs, the way it was so easy to distinguish from the steamy dampness over the rest of her body. It was a darker wetness, a deeper kind of heat. She moved slightly on the cotton towel on the bench and let her vaginal muscles contract stealthily. The discretion of female sexuality, its secret demureness, its endless interiority—in her case, particularly so. Yes, it was secret—solitary and contained at all times.

"Speak," he said. "Breathe and empty yourself." How could she? She could say she was thinking of his hands on her breasts—or how she hadn't been touched in that way in so long. (Was it truly years? Why was everything in her life suddenly measurable in years? Years seemed like months, months like weeks.) How long had it been? Since she saw Michael in the hospital. No, but that would be a nice fantasy to stick with, something she could almost make true by sheer will. Why not, if that's better than the truth. More truthful than the truth. No, the last one was Dean, of course. His name gave her an inward wince. Lorene told herself there was nothing to be ashamed of—she should regret nothing. But Dean was as far from Michael as possible, as uncomplicated and unmindful as they come. But that was a fantasy, too. She hadn't wanted Dean because he was the opposite of Michael. She had wanted Dean because he was great-looking and edgy and aloof and a bit nasty. It was her vanity. She found him very sexy.

Mina took only forty-five minutes to finish the walk to the hotel on Wilshire. She was, of course, late to meet Scott. She had never gone from Max to Scott on the same day. She was pretty sure she wouldn't like it, but she had to walk some-where—she didn't want to be home or at work. And she felt needed by Scott. Max hardly touched her anymore anyway. She wanted Scott's devotion. He was there at the bar, waiting, obviously relieved to see her. It was touching, almost, his order-ing a drink for her, clutching her hand, acting as if his good luck would be snatched from him at any moment, or if he might be arrested for desire or pleasure. It was endlessly appeal-ing, but then she felt sorry for him, and removed and suddenly bored. Here's the drink, now what to say? Drink it fast, get it in your head.

Lorene had slept with Dean and then feigned indifference. Dean flirted with her friends and seemed to hardly notice. Then they would collide through all the rooms in Lorene's apartment, having frenzied, intense movie sex. Sometimes

Dean would leave before dawn. It went on for several months. But the sex wasn't really good. It was department-store-lingerie, *Cosmo*-quiz tacky sex: it satisfied briefly and then bored her completely. And when she no longer wanted Dean, it wasn't gradual. It went all at once, with no warning. She just felt irritation and a vague revulsion in his presence. He didn't read that right, he thought it was part of their game. It worried her—that he didn't realize things had come to an end. He pursued her anyway. He began to hang around her restaurants. She ignored him and was utterly unresponsive. He began to sleep with her waitresses. Lorene wondered if he spoke about her, about the sex they had had. She started to feel the price of things, of the way he was still in her life even if she didn't want him to be. The low-grade menace of it—because surely by now he saw it was no game and he just lingered out of spite. She felt the weight of not being able to make ex-lovers disappear. It amazed her that Mina managed so well. Without all this bulimic self-reproach.

The last time she saw Dean he had wandered into Dead Animals and Single Malts at around eleven o'clock. He was already obviously drunk. He stood by the bar and watched her, in his black expensive suit, his dumb overly fashionable shoes and vapid smile. She couldn't bear men who wore fashionable shoes, unless, of course, they were gay men. He gave her heavy looks that irritated her completely—she almost felt bad for him. Almost. He had a drink and then grabbed her arm as she walked by. He pulled her over. That was it. She yanked her arm away.

"Look, Dean, I've had it. I don't want you touching me, or hanging out in my restaurants. I am not enjoying this and I want you to leave, now."

He smiled at her. "Lorene, Lorene, why are you such a little bitch?" When he spoke she realized he was more drunk than she had first guessed—there was an underslur to his speech, just the way the *ch* of *such* in a slushy, ugly, sloppy sound ran through the barely detectable *a* and became the *li* of *little*. *Sushalille*. This gave her some alarm. She hated drunk people, they became so narrow-focused and insatiable. Relentless. But to her surprise he let go of her arm and asked the bartender for his check. He put a bill of large denomination on the table and waved at the bartender to keep the rest. Lorene supposed Dean thought this gesture indicated class of some kind. She watched him leave. Dean had good, snaky hips, a nice long, graceful body. But as soon as he spoke or even gestured, all that dumb-boy vanity poured out. She felt something hard and cold inside her that she hadn't felt before. Dean was the last lover she'd had. It was such a shame. But she wasn't built for it, the combustible, vaguely menacing qualities. She felt nauseous thinking about it.

Mina straddled Scott's lap with all her clothes on. She felt his wanting her. She wanted him to slowly pull her skirt up, for them to kiss and feel each other up like schoolkids, not taking off their clothes until the last minute. But he just kissed her the way he always did, sort of perfunctorily and already wanting to be on to the next part, moving to the bed and taking off all his clothes.

"If you just want to wait until you're ready, that's fine. Just remember that until you speak, the healing cannot begin." Beryl applied pressure to her back, a steady touch that seemed to melt the aching in her shoulders. Lorene found herself talking aloud.

"I don't know what to say," she said. Beryl pressed her neck.

"I feel fear in your body, Lorene. Some deep fear. Tell me about that. Tell me what you fear. Be specific, and just go on, don't think too much."

Scott wanted to have dinner. He wanted to keep it going. She realized as she dressed that things had kept accruing for him. She had stayed in the same place all these months while he kept going deeper and deeper in. She felt a wind of panic. He said they had some things to discuss. She insisted no on dinner, she had to leave, was already late. She finally agreed to meet him the next afternoon. She agreed just to escape. She walked home, thinking tomorrow had to be the last time with Scott. She would have to tell him it was over.

"When I was walking from my car to this building, I passed a group of four guys huddled by their car. I think they were about eighteen years old. I readied myself for their staring. I readied the glassy gaze I have used my entire life. I saw peripherally a glance in my direction, and then I looked at one of them, but he wasn't looking at me. His gaze traveled right past me. He was completely indifferent to me. No look back. He gave me no look back. And I can't believe it. I am only thirty-two, and I am invisible to this guy. And then suddenly I saw the rest of my life stretched out before me. In a flash. The slow, excruciating dismantling of me as an object of desire. I would no longer command desire. And I felt so upset by this future, I wanted to run home and hide under my covers and cry. I really don't think I can bear it, you know, getting older." Lorene started to sob a bit, and Beryl held her shoulders.

"But that's not it. That's not what I'm afraid of."

"What then?"

"I am so scared that I am the sort of person who can be undone by such a thing. I'm so scared my whole life is built on something so inevitably doomed and so, well, so silly. I have spent the first third of my life fending off mostly unwanted attention from strangers, and I would spend the last two thirds pining desperately for that attention when it is gone. Now, that really scares the shit out of me."

Third Road Stop: New Mexico

Miraculously, Lorene wants to eat breakfast. Lorene wants to sit down and eat breakfast. I watch her eating pancakes with maple syrup. I watch her poke a fork into a sausage link. We discuss our plans to reach my mother's by the end of the week. I've already lost interest in open spaces. I urge her to the car. Lorene's eating a fucking sausage. Tentatively at first, then with gusto. Lorene's lips are glassy with sausage grease.

"I'm tired of driving," she says. "Can't we have another cup of coffee."

"No. I'll drive."

Lorene looks at me oddly.

"What. I said I'll drive," I say. She's wiping syrup off her unmade-up face. She looks so young. "You're kind of a mess this morning."

She smiles at me, licking her lips—it's breathtaking really.

"One more cup of coffee, doll, and then you can drive your heart out." She winks. I nod. I look for the waitress. She's talking to a young man furiously scribbling in a notebook. He looks up at her, hunted and unhappy, his hand shielding the page.

"There are people in the world who furiously scribble in notebooks, and then there are—"

"And then there are the rest of us. Unconcerned and undire," Lorene says, mouth full.

"Yeah, I guess. After Michael went to the hospital, he would send me things, documents, I guess." This is the first time I have mentioned Michael on our trip.

"After you wouldn't see him? What do you mean, documents?"

"Well, printouts from his computer, really. Not letters at all. Just fragments. Obsessive, odd, third-person diatribes. Which was really strange—obsessed but detached at the same time."

"I never got anything like that."

"Well, he spared you that. Only his family got the full force of his rants. And I did see him at the hospital. I did once."

"I know you did, Mina. At least he wanted to see you."

"I'm his sister, for God's sake."

I keep the cryptic notes in a drawer by my bed. With the postcards. Sometimes, I admit, I didn't even read them. They never had a salutation. They seemed to be dispatches from the front.

Fuck 'em, that's what they deserve. Damn sick of all these god-damn mediocrities. They don't understand, they don't want to understand. He frightened them, reminded them of what sellouts they are, rubbed their noses in the vapidity of their lives. They cannot deal with truths or truthsayers. He would be burned for this. He was certain they would kill him for these thoughts. They had designed it all very nicely, the benign smiles, the concerned

*looks. The restricted visits from family. His sister. Perhaps they
even got her. And then bringing the goddamn machine in here.
They wanted him to write again. Type his brain into electronic
bleeps that transmit through the computer into the universe.
What happens, he wondered, as he typed, to the deleted words.
The cursor blinking highlighted blips that seemingly flash into
erased nonexistence at the press of the delete button. Why was
this button twice as large as any of the letter buttons. What
deleted bytes of memory stay in electronic limbo. We can discover
the technology to recover data you deleted years ago. A search
engine with a thousand spiders crawling everywhere. It's all
there, somehow. Like a brain, imprinted, retained, waiting for
the recall. The right technology. He thought of abandoned hard
drives. He thought of landfills full of abandoned outdated computers. He thought of motherboards and microchips. Of punk
hackers in the future, constructing twisted, scavenged PC's from
the outdated abandoned stuff. Hybrid invasive technology.*

*They monitored his monitor. He created passwords. Data
alarms and hidden doorways of information. But if they monitored his creating these security measures, how could he protect
himself? They unleashed relentless, single-focused programs that
worked all day and all night to defeat his codes. Or even if he disconnected from all networks, all on-line communiqués (which he
did, because if information can come in, information can go out,
his data sucked out into the World Wide Web, replicated, dis-
seminated in a thousand ways, in seconds, without him knowing
a thing), there was still the plug, which sent electrical waves to
his computer. Suppose information could travel on those electronic pathways. He saw an endless stream of letters and words,
periods and commas, dashes and hyphens, streaming through
the walls, through outlets, into some mother monitoring com-*

puter. Then a printer spitting the reassembled bits out and into his file for everyone to scrutinize. No wonder they always said, *Write, write*. Stealing his secrets. Every time he deleted a word or a sentence or a paragraph, he would feel them vacuum through the cord, to the socket and the wall. He could hear a slight electronic whisper of usurped data. At night when he slept, or tried to sleep, he could hear the whir of words whispering through the wires in his walls. Everything he deleted lived on and on, every night whispering. It's the open sockets, that's why he can hear it. They think he's odd for putting tape over the socket holes. He can't stand all those electronic waves flowing into the room. Now they poured back into his computer.

One day he'll find a document, a story, composed of nothing but all the deletions he ever made, every random mistype, every dead-ended thought, every mistaken step, every regretted turn. All of his forgotten failures, assembled together, there on the screen.

He would have to take care of their computer. He knew now. He would delete what he really wanted to keep, and only "save" his mistakes.

Ibidem, Ad Libitum, Idem.

I kept all his "letters." For some unknown purpose.

At first it was a small heart-shaped bruise along the inside edge of forefinger and thumb. Mina noticed it as David sliced an apple, and then only in a certain light.

"How did you do that?" she asked. It was curious, the way she didn't hesitate to ask, how injuries are public, how one never hesitates to ask, *Hey, how'd you get that?*—it seemed to Mina, at this moment, oddly intimate.

"This?" David said, shrugging and smiling. "I'm clumsy. I fell running and jammed my hand."

Later she noticed on the far side of the bruised hand a thin red raised line. It was a cut, a red-pink-edged swell on his knuckle. She didn't ask about the cut (but it's more of a scratch, isn't it) but spent a moment or two contemplating the physics of falls. She tried to determine the contact order, the single-bullet theory of bruises—one fall or two? Gravel or pavement? Thumb then knuckle, or the other way around, or both at once or what?

"Do we have to do this?" she said. She opened a bag of chips and a powdered cheese puff of air escaped. The smell alone made her thirsty.

"We always do this. This is what we do. This is the day we do this. Don't act like Susan," he said, invoking the stay-at-home, invisible, despised girlfriend of one of their regular guests. He slid day-old snow peas out of a cardboard carton. He opened the carton of congealed rice and upended it. It came out in a glutinous mass, carton shaped. He slapped at it with the back of a plastic serving spoon. Slipft, slipft, slipft. It molded down into lumpy crags.

"Maybe I won't play tonight," Mina said. Dumplings, wet-looking and misshapen, thunked onto another plate. "What meat is in those, do you think? It looks gross," she said.

"You'll play. You always play. Don't do this every week. You always have fun, once you're into it. I can't always get you to get into it."

"I could just watch and not play," Mina said.

"It's the same meat in there as last night when you ate two and loved it," David said.

"I'll play but not for long," she said. He was dumping ice into the ice bucket. Getting out his cocktail shaker. The chilled martini glasses. Cutting twists.

"Gosh, you're good at cutting twists," she said. "Even with that scratch. I mean, the lemon might make the scratch sting."

"We could get pizza, I mean if this isn't good. Max could bring pizza."

She left the kitchen and examined yesterday's mail by the phone. There were two postcards. One was addressed to David:

"Wanton, Wary and Weary"
an episode of Eros and Others
teleplay by Max Mitchell
airing August 15 at 8pm on FOX

This card she threw in the garbage after tearing it into six equal pieces. The other card she did not read but put into her jeans pocket. It was addressed to her and she could feel the origin of it. Martinis, she really wanted one of David's ice-cold martinis out of his etched-glass vintage cocktail shaker. She watched him pour as people arrived. He handed one to her and it pleased her, to be offered something by her husband, and she didn't mind at all when he sat next to her and she could admire his smile and good spirits sideways, as he addressed his friends. He was nice to watch like this, perfectly OK. After she felt the cold heat of the thick, chilled vodka, she decided she would play. Poker, charades, Scrabble. Whatever game night entailed this week. Whatever sort of drunken ironic stupid excuse it took. Sometimes it was all just goofy calls in the poker ring, blind three-card stud with all ladies wild. Or baseball, at night, follow jacks, until they outdid one another with ridiculousness. Eventually, at some time during the evening—in the duration of the evening—you could slowly sense the serious shift in the game. Nearly undetectably, and sort of contagiously, people would start really trying to win, really wanting to win, and somebody would argue about somebody leaving, and somebody would tell someone they're taking it too seriously, and then Mina would think if she didn't live there, it certainly would be a nice time to leave. She would yawn, and start to clean up, and eventually go to bed, leaving them laughing and arguing. Tonight she couldn't wait for Max to arrive, and then studiously avoided any conversation that might address or exclude him. He behaved the same as always. He looked sexy, unshaven but combed, and in good cheer. She left for her room at eleven and undressed for bed. The next day he would probably call her at work and tell her, "I wanted to follow you in there, wanted to get under your Sunday nightie, press at you through the cotton until you woke up, and I'd have to cover your mouth when you came so the others couldn't hear us," or something like that, and she would wonder whether she should believe him. But the point was just the phone call and talking about it, anyway. It would make the work night bearable.

The other card, unfolded at last, read: *I want to see you. I miss you. It's suffocating on the road out in the world. PS I left the hospital and am heading east. All manner of dire request for your company on this expedition. Do not tarry. Do not pass go. Do not ignore me or you may not exist. Do not call or write. Just come here. Will be at Mom's in New York by September.*

Fidei Defensor, Michael

*   *   *

VIDEO #3

TITLE: MORE

GIRL on bed, legs crossed. Black-and-white, wobble-trembly, handheld.

> ### MAX (O.S.)
> You just talk about it.

GIRL puts her finger to her lips. She rubs her nail along the fleshy part of her lower lip, back and forth.

> ### MAX (O.S.)
> Stop that.

She looks at him, absent, continuing with her lip rubbing.

> ### MAX (O.S.)
> With the lip, stop. Get your fingers away from
> your mouth.

She stops, pulls her fingers away, and bites her lip in embarrassment, then she shrugs and sheepishly half-smiles.

> ### MINA
> Are you directing me? That's exciting. (*Pause.*)
> It's a habit. Do you ever wonder how it is that
> near-absentminded "nervous" habits offer so
> much comfort, but the comfort is only realized
> or thought of or appreciated after someone

orders you to stop? People flat out bark at you to stop as if they were saving you from some horrible mutilation, some regressive slide into nervous adolescence or an inadvertent pronouncement of neurosis. As if they were helping you. But it just gets on people's nerves. It irks them. It grates.

> MAX (O.S.)
> You're too self-conscious. Relax.

> MINA
> I can't relax. I'm too self-conscious.

Abrupt cut to a close-up of GIRL's hand. She massages the palm of one of her hands while staring at her thumb, wrinkling her flesh. Then the camera pans slowly up her body back to her face.

> MINA
> Can you really massage yourself? Does the pleasure of it derive from being acted upon by another body? Or is it like masturbation, where the fact that you know exactly what feels good almost makes up for the fact you have to do it yourself?

> MAX (O.S.)
> You don't have to speak.

Abruptly stops rubbing.

MINA

No, it's not like masturbation. It really isn't
satisfying to give yourself a massage.

GIRL just sits there. She yawns.

MAX (O.S.)

Mina, tell me. What's in your head, this
second?

MINA

Nothing, truly, there is nothing, just
embarrassment, and beyond that a wish to
please you, and beyond that, some real anger
and hostility.

MAX (O.S.)

Just stop talking about your feelings, and tell me
your thoughts, your random thoughts.

MINA

Hostility at you, at your trapping me here like this.

MAX (O.S.)

You just say the sentences in your head, the
phrases, whatever. You don't sum, don't make it
analytical.

MINA

I would say the hostility is paramount, it's really
the main thing at this point. I mean over the

desire to please and the embarrassment and the anger. If one wanted to construct a sort of hierarchy of emotion.

MAX (O.S.)

Mina.

MINA

I mean, to think that my vanity would allow me to accept the horrendous terms of being on the wrong end of a camera. To think I might enjoy the attention, your amplified attention. To be literally objectified and directed and exposed. Willingly manipulated only to discover later I really am ugly, really chew my lip like a ward case, really lose my chin when I laugh.

The camera moves into extreme close-up of her mouth, distorting her face, then abruptly cuts to her hands again, then back to her face. She seems animated, hyped up, excited by the noises coming out of her mouth.

MINA

There are a thousand little things one has no idea of, I mean in terms of how we come across. A gaze in the mirror is nothing. A gaze in the mirror is like a glance. A controlled moment of self-regard, a necessarily fixed thing. You only see yourself looking. But to be seen animated, looking down, looking away, talking, moving, is another world. All the thousand details of how

you move through any gesture, the true horror
of your own exposed humanness, the thousand
ways you give yourself away, off guard. And of
the thousand, nine hundred are ugly. At least
nine hundred or so are easily unattractive, if not
repulsive. And the sad thing—

MAX (O.S.)

It's about letting go of camera awareness. It's
about telling the truth. The truth is interesting.

MINA

The sad thing is you realize it has to be sort of
petty vanity that got you here in the first place,
in this disgusting position. And you can't resist
it. Disgust, hostility still, but mostly disgust.

The camera wobbles a little. Then it is a static shot from a
tripod. She looks off to the left, where the cameraman has
moved, still off screen, but apparently away from the camera.

MAX (O.S.)

The only thing that doesn't work, Mina, the only
thing that fails on camera is to be uninteresting.
Boring people. The easiest way to be interesting
is to tell the truth. The harder, deeper, more
vicious the truth, the more fascinating. That is it,
fascination, that's what the camera loves.

GIRL pulls out a cigarette. Max throws her a lighter from off
camera.

                    MAX (O.S.)
Abstracted pontificating about the nature of the
camera's gaze is not fascinating. Much, much
more difficult to fascinate if you try something
fancy. Much easier to bore.

She shakes her head, smiling.

                    MINA
Hostility, Max, huge mountains of nonabstract
anger and hostility.

                    MAX (O.S.)
Hmm. You might shut up. Or you might not.
This is the suspense, the narrative drive of this
video. Will she ever shut the fuck up?

                    MINA
Max?

                    MINA
The camera still on?

                    MAX (O.S.)
'Course.

                    MINA
You could turn it off. You could just come over
to the bed and see what happens.

                    MAX (O.S.)

Not yet.

She sighs.

                    MAX (O.S.)

Mina.

                    MINA

Yeah?

                    MAX (O.S.)

If you don't want to talk about yourself, if you
don't want to unveil your inner heart, you could
just do what you did before and undress.

                    MINA

You want me to take off my clothes?

                    MAX (O.S.)

Yeah.

                    MINA

Max, I think I might just do that. I think it might
be easier.

Mina starts to unbutton her dress.

                    TITLE: END

                *   *   *

Mina arrived at the Gentleman's Club to meet Lorene a miraculous hour early. She hadn't slept well. She spoke to David on the phone. She ordered a "drink." She did not think about Scott. She bused a few tables through the lunch rush. Her floor rhythm was off. She dropped things. She was annoying the wait staff. She almost called Max. She spent ten minutes changing the arrangement of salt and pepper shakers, moving them to the other side of the tiny vintage vases (several tea roses in each). She examined the tables. She returned the salt shakers to their original positions. She thought she might cry if spoken to.

She ate a dinner-sized lunch: a whole red snapper, so she could filet the fish, the odd and solid satisfaction of cutting off the head, then making the incision through the skin to the bone. A delicate touch is required, and the fish must be properly cooked. But it was something she knew how to do flawlessly. It felt very satisfying to put her fork along and under the sides of the incision, flicking back the halves of the fish intact and then, with the fork and knife, pulling up the spine from the end and removing it unbroken, in one deft gesture. It calmed her to do this one delicate thing.

When Lorene finally arrived, she had two men with her: a slender and beatific man Mina hadn't seen before and the high-voiced, thin-limbed Mariott, Lorene's restaurant designer. Mina watched as Lorene led the beatific man around the restaurant. He gestured at corners and windows. Mariott took notes, nodding and smiling. Mina approached them.

"Feng shui is all about placement of objects in a room for maximum peace and productivity," the man said.

"Lovely Mina, I want you to meet Beryl." Lorene winked at Mina.

"The energy flows would make this table the worst table."

"See, Mina? I told you nobody likes table twenty-three. I hate table twenty-three."

"What is this?" Mina said, gesturing to a chart in Lorene's hand. It was vibrantly colored and quite mathematical-looking.

Lorene handed it to her.

"It's a new astrological chart for the restaurant. Chinese and Indian astrology combined in one chart."

"A Chin-In horoscope."

"And this part is the feng shui analysis of the seating. It's going to help us with priority table placements."

"You want me to redo the seating according to this?"

"If you wouldn't mind."

Mina rolled her eyes.

"I used to work in an Italian restaurant, and when it was slow the owner made us go outside the front of the restaurant and toss salt. To get rid of evil spirits."

"Did it work?" Mina asked.

"Well, it gave us something to do other than stand there wondering why we were slow."

"A reason and a cure."

"Magical thinking and conjuring can be a great comfort, Mina. You shouldn't be so cynical about it."

Mina sat at the bar and took a sip of her soda. "Baby, somebody has to be around here. Or we are all liable to float into space. And then who would run the restaurant."

Lorene took a sip out of Mina's glass. "We'll finish this discussion later. Jake wants to meet with us now."

Mina sipped club soda and listened to Jake, the new floor manager of the Gentleman's Club, pitch bar concepts to Lorene. Lorene wore gold-rimmed oval glasses. The lens color was smoky amber. She wore a white Chinese heavy silk dress so tight that she had to lean rather than sit on the barstool.

"I don't know, tell Mina. Mina, listen to Jake. Ray, give me—what is Mina drinking?" she said.

"A Jeanne Crain Colada," Ray said, filling a glass with club soda.

"Ugh. Really? Fine, give me a Linda Darnell Daiquiri. Jake, talk."

Jake wore a sharkskin zoot suit, silver and cut as conservatively as a suit could be cut and still be called a zoot suit. He had *L-O-V-E* tattooed on his left knuckles, *L-I-K-E* tattooed on his right knuckles. After she hired him, Lorene speculated he had *I-N-D-I-F-F-E-R-E-N-C-E* tattooed on his cock. Mina liked the fact that Lorene said the word *cock* from time to time, and never said dick or penis or, even worse, made vague southbound hand gestures accompanied by a giggle.

"I have a couple of concepts which I know Lorene has heard and dismissed for various reasons before, but you, Mina, must convince her." Mina nodded, looked around the room, already bored.

"Cyber and Silk, a high-end Internet bar and restaurant. Everyone sees the success of cyber cafes; well, this would be a three-star-level cyber establishment." Jake was making room for himself as he launched into the pitch. Lorene removed her glasses. She held up a finger.

"No, and I'll tell you why," Lorene said, her lips matte auburn in the gold-tinged light. The lighting in all of Lorene's establishments was designed by the most respected Hollywood glamour technicians, and advertised as such. The back of the bar menu had credits to match any film, and her places got voted Most Flattering Lighting by the *L.A. Reader* three years in a row. That fact alone gave her enormous advantage over her competitors.

"But cyber places," Jake said. "Someone has to take it to the next step."

"Oh, cyber anything is so passé. Especially that word *cyber*. Totally over," Mina said.

"Yes, and especially not for Pleasure Model Enterprises. You see, this cyber crap is a fad. Fine. But it's not even social. The whole point of the Internet is not to be seen but to be comfortably agoraphobic, to travel without moving, to interact without contact—precisely the opposite of my philosophy of contemporary social enterprise. I create social clubs—for company. Not techno-pseudo company, but actual human company. Dietary fetish—fine. I want to create environments for people to indulge safely, not regress to cubicles of self-involvement. And, God, the idea of computers, possibly the ugliest design objects on earth, in one of my restaurants, and that horrible green-tinged light they give off, right on people's faces—oh, God." Lorene put her glasses back on.

"But it goes with your contradiction theory—social but antisocial at the same time," Mina said.

"Yes, but some things are not appropriate for public space. Masturbation is fun, but the point of it is its privacy. I wouldn't have masturbation bars. Next idea, Jake. What have you been up to, Mina, you're flushed."

"OK. Incense and Peppermints, a surreal retro sixties club. Sort of Dada–*Clockwork Orange*. White plastic. Call the food 'strawberry steak shortcake,' that sort of thing. Or munchies drug food, Oreos and peanut butter sandwiches. Potato chips and ice cream. Saltines and ketchup. Furry teacups, that sort of thing."

Lorene shook her head. Mina shuddered.

"Nice stockings, Mina," Lorene said. Mina extended one oatmeal-colored cashmere leg against Lorene's silk-covered thigh. Lorene put one manicured hand on Mina's knee.

"Oh, my. Yes. Cashmere. Wow. Cashmere cable knit, no less. Very sort of Ali MacGraw-ish, I think."

"That's what I was going for."

"OK, one more idea," Jake said, and the women turned to him. He took one of Lorene's cigarettes and Mina lit it for him.

"We call it Blow Up. A sort of Antonioni-inspired milieu where model-perfect indifferent women are draped about in various throes of ennui and the food takes a really long time to come to your table."

"Maybe it never comes," Mina said, and all three of them started to smirk.

"OK, OK, I'll work on other ideas." Jake shook his head, laughing.

"Really, you're getting closer, Jake. Just remember, it actually has to be pleasurable as well as high-concept. Pleasure."

"Are there really throes of ennui?" Mina said, touching her stocking.

Lorene shook her head. "He's too awful. Completely tragic." They watched Jake shrug away and retreat to the floor, where the one o'clock rush was suddenly upon him.

"I got a postcard from Michael," Lorene said. Mina drained her glass.

"Yeah, I know, I know. Jesus. I don't want to talk about it."

"You want another drink?" Ray asked them.

"Yes," Mina said. "Something red."

"An NC-17, straight up."

"I forgot, does that get fruit?" Ray asked, lining up the glasses.

"Natch."

Lorene and Michael. Mina met Lorene through Michael. Only after Michael was gone from L.A. did they become friends, years after they had met for three seconds, it seemed to Mina, at a party her suddenly grown-up brother had thrown for her at their father's house in L.A. After the first school year they had spent apart, Mina at boarding school, Michael in L.A. at an art school for gifted youth.

Mina had spent most of that night sitting on the stairs, feeling lumpen and fourteen, examining the crowd. A party, she thought. This is one of those strange parties like you see in movies from the seventies; there was something plastic and explosive and inevitable about it, with the odd L.A. retro lightweight irony that went as far as how you dressed—flapper dresses with clear plastic go-go boots. Nineteen seventy-nine punk bondage pants with a pink tube top. Sixties op-art minidresses with combat boots. S&M stilettos with dyke hiphop jeans and Twiggy-lined kohl eyes. It was six decades of fashion mistakes all juxtaposed, recontextualized, "deconstructed" by people who really believed fashion was the heart of subversion. Not the badge, not the consequence, but subversion itself was found in a Bakelite bracelet on a tattooed wrist. She felt both superior to this and deathly envious, the way she felt about fashion in general, longing for days of Catholic-schoolgirl uniforms, blue-skirted and neutral. She wanted uniforms, fascism of some kind, to take away the tinkling, enticing fashion distraction. Brown shirts and sackcloths. Then we'll see what you have to do to be subversive. Not piercing and tattooing, I tell you. She was nearly mumbling to herself about this when Michael interrupted with a squeeze on her arm.

"I remember when I first started seventh grade. It was the

height of punk. British class war hit suburban L.A. and transformed into a beautiful mall-driven, middle-class American nihilism. Everyone said shave your head, pierce your nose, mutilate yourself to prove you're not just a weekend rebel. Make yourself unhirable, undesirable. But now it is desirable, and practically required for hire. It is absorbed and digested, thrown in your face to mock you. It makes me feel old." Michael smiled, seventeen and handsome, a closed-mouth and sheepish grin. He had the disturbing habit of nearly reading her mind. She put her face on his shoulder.

"You have such cool parties, Michael," she said.

"It's your party. You could actually, you know, sort of walk around, talk to people. I threw it for you."

"Yeah, threw it in my face." She leaned on him as if he was a fifties boyfriend—a man's chest felt fantastic when it was a place you could look up and out from, the whole world at a distance from the weight of your head. He put his hand in her hair.

"What's wrong? Are you just sleepy, or do you want to talk about it?"

"What? Oh, no. My psyche feels like it shrank in the wash and now the edges don't quite reach anymore. It's a coverage problem."

He stroked her hair and the side of her face. His fingers felt soft and light-touched. An incredible gentleness. He pulled her down the stairs and abandoned her at the cocktail table. She moved to the edge of the bar, her mouth smiling and slightly open. She poured some vodka in a highball glass, some cream, then some Kahlúa. She drank it down fast. Like ice cream. She poured another, feeling something classic and teenage take hold of her, an archetype setting in. Drunk. Party. She watched vinyl and satin and leather go by, spikes and skin, and she felt almost sexy and slightly removed. She stared down, looking at her feet in low-heeled leather boots. She groaned. Got to stop dressing like such a dyke, swear it. Jeans and boots and these goddamned baggy shirts, oversized and softly worn through. No makeup and long, straight blond hair. A fucking yogurt commercial, a Pepsi commercial, a goddamned milk ad. She shuddered.

"You seem to be having an interesting conversation with yourself."

Mina jumped at this, caught, smiled at the speaker.

"You're reading yourself the riot act?"

Mina had never seen this woman before. She had certainly not noticed her all night. She was a bit older than most of the people at the party. She wore a long fur coat, leopard skin, ankle length. It had not-too-stylized shoulder pads and was tapered to the waist. Mina would date it about the late thirties. Her hair was black and combed sleek and shiny at shoulder length. It was parted at the side rather dramatically. Cyd Charisse meets young Joan Crawford. Vixen hair. And she had the delicate small features that people would call "doll-like and porcelain," but hers actually were porcelain and doll-like.

"Is that a real leopard-skin coat?" Mina asked.

"Of course. Feel it," she said. Mina looked at the glossy soft sleeve, the deep black and warm orange-gold colors. It made her hair look ebony, blue-black, Superman-comic-book black. This in turn made her skin whiter. She examined her hands, white and manicured and red-nail painted. She looked at her feet. Pumps with sheer black stockings. She wondered about seams. She wondered what her dress was like under the coat. The coat, my God, the coat.

"No, thank you. It looks real, I've just never seen one before."

"If you've never seen one before, how do you know it looks real?" She smiled and looked in Mina's eyes.

"It's like too beautiful not to be real," she said. The doll woman laughed and laughed. She had one of those condescending, amused laughs, knowing but genuine. Mina liked it. Mina liked her condescension. She was sure this woman did know more than she. More about everything in the whole world. All she could think was, Good, I made her laugh.

"If you think it looks beautiful, you ought to feel it," she said quietly. She held out a fur-covered arm.

"Oh, no, I can't do that. I'm sure it's great, it's best if I don't touch it. I'll just look from afar."

"That's wise. If you touched it, you might be overcome with a desire to get your own, and coats like this one are very rare. Very, very rare."

"Yes, I'm sure. I think you actually get crucified in some parts of the city for wearing a coat like that. Don't they like force you to register with the police when you move into a new area, with the sex offenders? Are you restricted to after-curfew hours so no small children see you? Aren't you like barred from whole arenas of employment possibilities? Do housewives burst into tears at the sight of you?"

The doll woman smiled and pulled out a long European cigarette. She held it near her mouth and stopped smiling. She looked down at Mina's feet, then back at her face. Perhaps she was trying to find something to comment on in her clothes. In any case, she kept it to herself, because she just looked at Mina with that near-smile. Mina supposed it was a vague sexual come-on, but couldn't be sure. She began giggling, and Mina was hopeless when she got nervous and got the giggles. The woman pursed her lips, about to say something. Mina continued to giggle.

"I'm sorry, I'm hopeless," Mina said, now breathless. The woman again seemed about to speak, and Mina suddenly came forth with another muffled guffaw, which she tried to extinguish in her mouth and instead created an actual snort. She had to admit, as embarrassing as the giggles were, as conscious as she was that her nervousness was causing the laughter, she did enjoy it. She couldn't stop because the laughter itself became funny, the way it sounded and felt in her body, it was hilarious. So she was trying to stop, but then she wasn't really. The woman finally smiled benignly, and then looked away, no longer about to speak. Michael approached and lit her cigarette. She smiled at him and he turned to Mina.

"Are you OK, Mina?" he asked.

"Me?" she said, and then it was gone, the laughing fit. She was exhausted and serious. "I'm OK."

"You met Lorene, I see," he said.

"Yes, sort of," Mina said.

"Lorene, this is my fantastically wonderful and much missed little sister."

Lorene smiled. She looked at Michael and then got very sad-looking. She touched his collar and smoothed it a little.

"Are you leaving?" he said. She nodded. Then walked away.

"Just don't ask, all right?" he said before she could even open her mouth. He was in a bad mood the rest of the night. It was years later, after Michael got sick, that Lorene called her and asked her to help her open her first restaurant. She knew it was Lorene's way of staying close to Michael, but she didn't mind. She wanted to be Lorene's close friend. She still wanted to be her close friend. And they hardly ever talked about Michael anymore.

It had to be the last meeting with Scott. She was supposed to meet him at the usual time, the usual place. Only this was the last time, she swore it. After all, she had done everything she could to contain it, made strict limitations. No phone calls. The Gentleman's Club's number in an emergency, because she "lived there, practically," and no discussion of her life. Her life was simply "complicated" and "private." And Scott had accepted these terms.

They would meet, have a drink. Just like yesterday, when she couldn't get the drink in her fast enough.

The month before she had almost ended it. It had started in the usual way with them. London, he would say. Bahrain. Taiwan. Singapore. Hotels. Dinners with clients. The lonely time-zone boy. Bonus and banks and Bedouins. Finance deals. Conference calls. She liked to hear the details of his banker's life. She found catalogs of his business details erotic. Then she would press him. How lonely were you? Did you get a massage? Did you have a Thai girl sent to your room? Scott would blush and deny it. She found it exciting to press him for sexy details. To untie his Southern gentility.

"Well, there was one time."

"When?"

"I was feeling awful, drunk, far from home. I ordered a massage."

"Charged to the bank, I hope." He put his index finger in his drink and stirred the ice a little, then put his finger in his mouth. Mina found the gesture an oddly feminine one. It was too overtly sensual for Scott, too contrived. She preferred him wound tight, audience to her own sexy gestures. But she had pressed him for details too many times, and now he was a little self-conscious in his revelations. It made her weary.

"She came to my room. Tiny, shy."

"Eyes averted," Mina said.

"Eyes averted." Scott smiled. Mina tried to picture it, but Scott's smile ruined it.

"Have you ever told anyone this before?"

"No, no, I haven't," he said. He took a sip of scotch. His usually very short hair had grown out a bit. He looked boyish, his eyes were sad. Mina suddenly felt it then, in that second, his sadness, and she wanted him again. She picked up his hand. He had large hands, the palms wide and the fingers in proportion, but elegantly formed, and the skin was soft and smooth.

"She had me undress and lie on the bed. She draped a towel over my hips and rubbed oil on me. She gave a slow, deep massage with tiny, strong hands."

Mina turned Scott's hand over and gave the lightest possible kiss to his inner wrist. She let her lips relax and catch a little as she moved them slowly on the pale veined skin. She moved over his palm to his fingers. She could taste a bit of salt, a bit of scotch. The tang of nicotine that tasted a bit like a woman to her. She thought of how after sex his fingers did smell like her. She imagined, even after a few hours and a shower, he might get a hint of sex on the airplane home when he rested his fingertips on his upper lip during a lull in conversation with the old lady from Greenville sitting next to him. Azaleas and spring, her unmarried niece. He blushes as the old woman talks, remembers how long a month is. When Mina thought of Scott like that, polite to the world, holding open doors and carrying coats but secretly overwhelmed, still kind of blushing—she'd think she could

marry Scott, take care of him, be wrapped in some perfect suburban dream of bourgeois sex and storybook Christmases. Her
secret desire to be Doris Day and normal came over her. It even
felt sexy to imagine him coming home from the office late,
smelling of another woman's perfume, guilt-ridden and skittish.
They would fight and have aggressive sex. But no, not likely. She
was confusing Scott and Max. Scott would just weep, probably,
confess everything and feel too guilty to touch her. She would
watch TV and eat fat-free cookies.

"She had massaged every part of me, and I'm nearly asleep
but nevertheless aroused," Scott said.

"Yes, are you on your back at this point or your front?"

"My back, towel draped over my cock."

"Are your eyes open or closed?"

"Open, definitely," he said.

"Men's eyes are always open, aren't they?"

"Pretty much, yeah," he said, watching Mina rub his fingers
almost absently across her lips.

"Is it sexier if the woman's eyes are open or closed?"

"You ask the strangest questions. It depends, I guess."

Mina looked up at him with a closed-mouth grin. "Do you
think these questions are sexy?"

"Umm. Yeah."

"You're on your back, towel draped across you, aroused."

"Yes," he said, shifting in his chair, looking sadder still and
down.

"What next?"

"She said, without looking at me, 'Massage?' and she
pointed at my toweled midsection. I nodded and she put her
hand under the towel and very quickly and expertly brought
me off," Scott said, pursing and grimacing his lips a little. "She

was quite efficient and matter-of-fact about it. It was, I admit, very pleasurable, a clinically precise and passive relief. There was, I think, a fifty-dollar charge on my hotel bill for the addendum hand job."

Mina thought it wasn't a sexy story at all, but it was undoubtedly true, and so ordinary and dull a little tale that she almost convinced herself she was in love with Scott, that she needed to wrap him in warm flesh for the rest of his days. But this was just because she had to end things with him, because she knew it would be one of the last times.

At dinner that night he had calculated the number of times. He had a financier's belief in interest and dividend, as though accumulated days guaranteed a return of some kind. He ordered a second bottle of wine. She let him. He spoke about his newly purchased house in Brooklyn Heights. Its authentic Federalist details. She didn't quite listen, but thought of the first time they ate together. How he took her coat for her. He pulled out the table for her when she stood and when she sat. She knew these gestures meant nothing, that politeness was just learned habit. Yet when he held open doors and pulled back chairs, she felt an undeniable comfort. It was a protocol that hinted at an intact fabric, an order, a world in which she would be safe. When he pulled the table back to ensure she sat more easily, when he concerned himself with ensuring her comfortable and frictionless glide through the world, it had an embarrassingly intoxicating and erotic effect on her. Mina realized, suddenly, that this was a date, that these were the gestures of an old-fashioned date. That he was not winking at gestures, not imitating a fifties movie or displaying anything but complete earnestness. She knew then she should tell him, warn him, but she didn't want to. Mina had never been on a date before.

That time he had spoken of a domestic life, a new life. He wanted to care for her and have her care for him. She smiled and touched his hand and said what she always said when he tried to escalate and accrue.

"But this is nice, isn't it? The way things are right now between us?" And Scott nodded and stopped talking and they went to his room and had undistinguished, comfortable sex. When he touched her these days, she had to think of Max, of a whispered word, of a forceful kiss. No way would Mina manage to be what Scott hoped she would be, even if she decided she really wanted it. No way.

No letters, she had said. She had tried in good faith to contain it, hadn't she? No gifts. No phone calls. But containment didn't really work, and there was a deepening asymmetry between them. It made their relations stagnant and lonely.

She was getting close to being late for today's assignation. (Lorene came up with names: assignation, rendezvous, tryst, bankers' meeting, ATM time, MI—monthly indiscretion. It was amazing how the more names Lorene came up with, the less Mina was able to give it serious regard. She felt guilty about that, guilty toward Scott, then guilty for her guilt, for pitying him.) She lingered at the restaurant.

Scott would be at the hotel bar, by himself. Ordering a second drink, maybe. Watching the door, glancing at his watch, certainly.

Mina left the restaurant. She walked past her favorite boutique on Beverly Boulevard. She wandered absently inside. She was really late now. She needed some new shoes. She needed black kid-leather sling-backs. Maybe open toed. She usually didn't go open toed. But sling-backs, or maybe mules. Black silk mules. Something Betty Grable-ish, something look-back-and-over-the-shoulder-ish. Something to sit in her closet for a lifetime, unworn except for three minutes in a boutique on Beverly Boulevard. Shopping is a form of daydreaming, a way to recast your life instantly, a desperate optimism about the meaning of style and detail. Such a fleeting feeling, but impossible to resist. She knew she was the kind of woman who couldn't walk past a post office without wanting to buy stamps.

Scott finished his second drink.

He'd have called the restaurant by now. On that awful little streamlined and lightweight cellular phone. To be interrupted at all times in all places is a contemporary privilege, privacy and exclusivity oddly inverted. Do you think people might figure that out, that all the underlings of the world might be forced to carry mobile phones, and the big bosses the only ones entitled to be unreachable?

No, definitely not sling-backs, but mules. She looked at her foot. Her instep. Even the word oozed sex: instep. When you walk in mules, your eyes go to the curve of the instep, the sudden nakedness of the secret underside of the foot, the way it promised things about your life.

She didn't make it to the bar. She went to the Gentleman's Club with her new purchase. Lorene sat at the bar with one of the night managers, Sam (real name Kenny).

"Mina, my love, what a surprise," Lorene said, patting the barstool next to her with a freshly manicured hand. Moroccan Mauve Lacquer in Cool Matte. One of Mina's least favorites. She sat, dazed, imagining she might just have a drink and a cigarette or two. She drew her packages on her lap. She liked the sound heavy paper boutique shopping bags made when they rubbed up against slick-coated cardboard such as an expensive shoe box. It sounded clean to her, and she liked it almost as much as the sound the boxes made when they were at last opened, the pulling up, the lifting of the whole of it until the bottom half slid apart with a moany, pregnant sound. Then the whispers of tissue, everything encased in matching colored tissue paper.

"Let's see what you got," Lorene said. Lorene placed the box on the bar top. She pulled out the perfectly formed mules, the raw black silk spotless and pristine. It was curvy and dangerous, a personality-altering shoe. One must feel a certain way in it. One must.

"A shoe like this could change your life, doll."

Mina put a finger on the vamp, the open-toe cap. Lorene looked at the shoe and then back at Mina's absent fondling. She frowned. Lorene knew how to read the gestures of women. Mina put the shoes away.

"I'll have a drink, Ray," Lorene said. "A Ward number six, please. Cuban style. Mina?"

"A club soda." She smirked at Lorene.

"You're no fun," Lorene said.

"I stood up Scott," Mina said.

"Yo, no kidding. I could tell from the shoes. Heart-trampling shoes."

"Did he call?"

"Just three times."

"Oh, God. I'll go over there. I should." Mina got up and pulled her hair back into a thirty-second ponytail, then dropped it.

"Hey, you forgot the shoes."

"You keep them," she said, nearly through the door, not looking back.

On Route:
Lubbock to New Orleans

"The first time you did it," she says.

We are escaping whole states on Route 10.

She has made me drive the long haul from Santa Fe to Houston, one unbreaking line, speeding through the flat brown Texas landscape, the air saturated with manure and dust. We had stopped miserably in Lubbock, found an off-brand ersatz Howard Johnson's where Lorene had eaten a butter-drenched gray twice-microed potato and I kept eyeing her cell phone on the table between us. We are going miles out of our way, on Route 10, to get to New Orleans. Lorene wants one girls' night out in the French Quarter, a forced idea that only grows less attractive the closer we come to it. I can't wait to get to the East Coast, my mother, some safe, sane place where I can consider myself. I couldn't get out of Texas fast enough, only finally relaxing into a driver's highway trance after we crossed the Sabine River.

"That's the subject," I say.

We have taken to asking questions with no inflections in our tone, a form of road disease that has come upon us simultaneously, and we adjust without speaking of it. It is an intimacy, the beginnings of a secret language, the way a journey makes you alien to everything but the journey itself.

"You have a better subject," she says.

"You mean the first time I had sex with someone. Loss of virginity. How I became a woman. We are that bored. No, don't answer that. But these are guaranteed dull stories."

"No, never dull. Guaranteed not dull."

"Look at Louisiana. Lorene, look—Louisiana. Bayou country. Below sea level. Slant-roofed shacks and mushy turnip gardens," I say.

Even from the leveling uniformity of the interstate a difference has settled in. Everything looks fetid and damp, sagging in the middle and abandoned. Things seem to be growing in the wrong places, more bacterial than lush, a huge petri dish where people could live only if they grew up here and had the proper biology.

"I don't like looking at landscape. I like people talking. I want some secret and intimate memory. Some human experience to make all this window-watching palatable," she says. Lorene has revealed her bar owner soul. She wants to hear the intimacies of others' lives as fill and distraction. She is not, as I had thought, a great listener, but instead an interrogator, an extractor of confession and disclosure. A verbal voyeur, I guess.

"You tell, then. What your first time was like," I say absently.

I see a man up ahead, sitting by the road. The road runs so flat and uncurved that I notice him as a dot and watch him grow larger and more in focus as we travel toward him. He, I suppose, watches us grow larger, and now we are nearly upon him as he sits, doing, I think, absolutely nothing, not hitchhiking or trying to cross or walk, but just sitting there, in a duster shirt untucked and loose jeans, his face caved in and sunbeat, his mouth working as if chewing or speaking. He is in a crouch, not sitting but squatting, and I realize that he is defecating, or trying to, but I can't be sure because of the shirttails and the speed at which we pass. As I glance at the rearview mirror, though, I think the posture unmistakable, and he continues, unaffected by our passing.

"I asked you first. I want to know, just tell me," she says, lighting a cigarette with the car lighter, the toasted cigarette paper clinging to the hot gray-red glow. It smells almost good — mittens, maybe, if you put them in the toaster.

"Your nail polish looks like hell," I say, gesturing with my chin at her lovely hands. The nail tips are showing white where the ever-shiny Perpetually Wet and Angry Anise purple-black has worn and chipped away. Her fingertips are bitten into Good & Plentys.

"Sorry," she says, clenching her hands and actually sounding sorry.

"You're not traveling well," I say.

"Shut up," she says.

"It's awful," I say, "it's depressing me." She actually looks quite beautiful, but I enjoy upsetting her, hectoring her a bit like some bully boyfriend. I find it sexy. She turns her head away from me at a sulky angle and stares out the window. We sit that way until I take the cigarette out of her hand and take a drag.

"All right, I'll tell you. Are you listening," I say.

Lorene is wearing a white T-shirt, and I don't think I've ever seen her in a T-shirt before. Her perfect C-cup breasts appear to be having an exceptional day. She is, of course, braless, the tightness of the T-shirt holding everything in place. Her nipples are smooth and darkly visible. I don't mind looking at them.

"I was fourteen. His name was Mal Ortensky. He was sixteen," I say.

"Mal," she says.

"We were on the same baseball team. He used to meet me after games and help me with my swing, with my arm, with my catch."

"You played catch," Lorene says.

"Yes, Mal. He took an interest in me. So one day he was standing behind me, helping me with my swing. You know, his hands were on my hands. His arms on my arms. He was standing behind me, talking in my ear. You get the picture," I say.

"Fourteen."

"Yes."

"Catch," she says, "his arms on your arms."

"Yes."

"Then what," she says.

"Well, these stories are pretty standard from there, aren't they."

"No, you could say where, and what was said and how it felt," Lorene says, "what you thought, what happened after."

"OK. Under the bleachers, after dark. He said nothing. It felt like nothing. A little pulling at first."

"Then. Seven seconds over Tokyo."

"No, he made me come eight times."

"Eight times in seven seconds."

"Pretty good for sixteen, huh," I say. She smiles through a weary giggle, examining her hands. She uses her thumbnail to peel bits of polish off her other nails. It has become her road project.

"I think I should have said more about breasts or thighs or something. Thrown in a detail about blood or how he kept his baseball cap on and it kept hitting my forehead."

"That's all right, though," she says. "The baseball stuff is kinda sexy, actually."

"Your turn."

Lorene does not stop picking her nails.

"You shouldn't have said under the bleachers."

"Your turn."

"You may as well have said in the backseat of his car, Mina."

"Your turn."

"OK, my turn."

Lorene doesn't say anything, but tilts her head in the way certain women do when they are making room for their thoughts. The way men tend to stand back to make room for their speech. She untilted. I see a shiny look come over her. She removes her sunglasses. The gesture exudes a wistful earnestness.

"It's difficult to explain," she begins.

"Lorene."

"I was eighteen."

"Lorene."

"What."

"Sorry about the bleachers."

She made it to the bar just as Scott was ready to leave.

It had never felt real to her. Not even a real betrayal of her husband, none of it real until this moment when she had to extract herself from his life.

The first time with Max, however, had felt absolutely a betrayal. Not even that, but the first real thought of it, and then the weeks when the thought wound its course to the first time and then a series of times. She had thought of Max, imagined them together, right in the kitchen while she washed dishes with David. While they rewound a video, in those whirring seconds of unoccupied time, or when they shopped, or, oh, yes, when they spoke of ordinary, Sunday things. She thought of Max. Especially then. David touched her, or put an arm around her, and she allowed herself to think what if it were Max's arm, and it made the act pleasurable for her. When they watched a good movie, and she noticed something she hadn't before—what was it? That movie where Joseph Cotton is the evil uncle—she didn't want to share her thoughts with David but wanted to tell Max. She made a mental note to tell Max. That was betrayal.

The actual doing was all fear of being caught and consequences—not any real line being crossed that hadn't already been crossed in her imagination. And when she felt her longing for Max while David smiled at her, at first she wanted to confess, to beg him to understand, to wear ashes, to burn her hair, anything. But instead she drove the feelings from her mind, did a sort of mental hygiene—this is one man, that is another—imagined she could will a compartmentalized life. And to her amazement, for a while, it worked. She could drive it out, nearly live in separate parts of herself. She felt her own power, and astonishment. She realized, coldly, ambivalently— she could do anything. She could do anything.

But now things had changed. Some feeling of vague agitation, anxiety. A worry she couldn't contain it and would make a blunder. Some horrible exposure. She would trip herself up, and in fact she sort of vaguely wished for it—some trip-up so she could at last be relieved of it. The external pressure, the nagging fatigue. Something in the notes from her brother was making those segues between one interaction and another longer and more difficult. Or the not driving, which made it impossible to move fast enough to not feel everything confused and out of her control and sure to collide. Or maybe it was the way Max's movies had quickly moved from the embellishment of their erotic life to becoming the thing itself. Or the way her triple life made her think everyone wasn't as they seemed, made her suspicious of David, of everyone. She knew she couldn't contain it any longer, hold it together.

Scott's face looked so shocked, so deeply unprepared. She spoke and as she spoke, she watched the words register on his face. She sounded dumb and mean. Not like a movie, not witty. But she had been so careful, so scrupulous. She had, hadn't she?

The compartments were breaking down.

Lisa scrubbed potatoes and carrots. She ran water over them as she scrubbed until they revealed tender bright colors, which would turn dull and gray after a long boiling. She soaked lettuce in bowls of water—raw vegetables made her nervous. She peeled and scrubbed and soaked and rinsed. It took hours. Mark hated how overboiled the vegetables came out. He was wrong, though, it had to be done. He didn't realize how delicate they were, how tiny children's bodies are, how vulnerable they all were. She made a meat sauce because Mark wanted meat. But the ground beef—she pressed it in the frying pan at a high temperature. The fat sizzled and popped at her wrists as she pressed down on the meat, separated the clumps. Pink was dangerous, she cooked it on high heat until it was nearly black and stunk of frying pan and burnt fat. She made sure every hidden thing in it was dead. *Stracc*-something, staph infection. *E. Coli*, with a number—so many strains of things they required numbers—triple digits. No, more—*E. Coli* 0157:H7. That was the superbad virulent supertoxic one. Six digits and with colons and letters, too. Then in with the cooked-out tomatoes, until everything tasted the same—safe. She felt like a cave woman, killing her food in the microbe hunting ground for the good of her family.

Mark hated her cooking.

But what could she do? *Listeria* and *Trichinella* and anti-
biotic-resistant superbacteria. Alex and Alisa set the table. They
reached up to place plates. She had made the meat sauce for
Mark, but Mark wouldn't be home. Mark hadn't been home in
two days. They began to eat quietly, in his absence, drinking distilled water as Mark's beer sat in the refrigerator. The food was
not tasteless; it tasted like Teflon and burnt toast. It tasted like a
textural lumpy mess. The kids didn't want it. Lisa yelled at them
to eat. They had to eat their vegetables. She made them cry.
Mark would not be back, she knew. She could make him, force
him back with guilt and pleading, but how long would it last?
And how much more living could they do with someone who
didn't want to be there, someone feeling trapped. One had to
choose; there wasn't enough in her for Mark and for Alex and
Alisa. Alex was screaming at her, he hated this dinner. She felt
in her son's voice the fear of change, and heard how much she
was to blame. Alisa sobbed, making girlish audible gulps for air.
Lisa started crying and got out the peanut butter and saltines.
I'm sorry, she said. I'm sorry, here. And the three of them ate the
crackers and the peanut butter.

"We'll have ice cream and chocolate sauce for dessert," Lisa
said. "OK?" The children nodded and ate, red-faced. Lisa
forced in the horrible food, putting pats of butter and fingerfuls
of salt on it. She also ate the peanut butter and the crackers.
She ate the ice cream with the chocolate sauce too, already
seeing the end of it as she ate, already wondering what conso-
lation was offered after ice cream. Her stomach felt uncom-
fortably large. It was so constantly full these days that she
couldn't hold it in at all. Her muscles a distant memory under
her fat, and it made her sad and hungry and tired. It felt per-

manent. It surrounded her, her body, weighed her down, but still she ate. Mark had to leave, and what could she do now? She would have to go to her mother's, be at the door with nothing but her children and her hunger. She could stay here only with Mark's support—there was no way she could make it without his money. They cleaned up the kitchen together, the children trying to dry the dishes with quiet, obedient faces. She had let them down, she was frightened. She let herself become unlovable, fat and ugly and messy, and because of this they had no father. They watched TV, and while the children couldn't see, she cried to herself. They ate the expensive store-bought cookies, and she wept. She was not crying about losing the apartment. She was crying now because she would not have Mark's arms around her in her bed, that she had lost that, too.

David wanted to take Gwen to the Getty Museum. He wanted to show her something marble and anciently solid. He wanted to look at her as she moved through the world. But Gwen wanted to confine their explorations to her bed. She grew strict with him without saying anything. Her containment was apparent to David in the smallest unspoken moments, a code he read and contemplated in his solitude at home, staring at his computer screen. He picked up a photograph on her mantel. Gwen's daughter, fat like Gwen, but sad and apologetic.

"What's your daughter's name?" he asked. She smiled halfway. A long pause.

"Come here," she said, as if giving up something valuable. He knew he should shut up and he did. He trusted her completely. She could undo him, not from across a room, but within body-heat distance. Or on the telephone. When he first spoke to her, she called him after reading one of his scripts. It was her job, not an extraordinary gesture in itself, but the minute he heard her voice, he felt she would help him somehow. When he first saw her, she seemed unappealing to him. He thought she looked uncomfortable in clothing, pulling at her sweater, burdened by largeness. But he liked her. She was both kind and commanding in her critiques of his work. She had confidence in her opinions. David felt relieved of things when he was near her. They often met at her West Los Angeles home. They would sit under a sun umbrella by a large and elaborate sycamore tree. One particular afternoon, no different-seeming from any of the others they had spent together, she moved out of the shade and into the sun. She undressed to complete nakedness and stepped into the shallow end of the pool. She was soft, fleshy, white. He watched as she waded in, moving slowly, graceful in the weighted way that some large women are. She waded out, approached him glistening with water. Her breasts seemed enormous to him, pendulous, but the skin perfect, perfectly white, the nipples pink and wet. She kissed him, that first time, and she was sweet-tasting, liquid, light.

She did not want to talk about the daughter or the husband. She was content in her life. But she wanted David, and it was not something he questioned, he wanted her back. She made him forget about movies. She made him think about women in paintings—a glossy book from college of elaborate, solid women. Or of carved, still women that didn't change when shadows overtook light and then back again. Women who inhabited one place in the world as you moved around them. He explored her curves, her Bernini twists and endless thighs. He kissed her dimpled spine, felt her muscular and soft flesh that gave when pressed, that didn't resist. He moved on top of her, his front to her back. He liked the way her neck smelled. This he was unused to, she was more than him, anchored and fecund on the bed. Things became elaborate in the way things that excluded everything else usually do. They became overly elaborated, from baroque to rococo. She had silky scarves, blindfolds. He was on the bed—she tied his hands to the bedposts. She covered his eyes. He felt liberated by trust. Things touched him. Intricate salty flesh on his mouth. He felt with his tongue—layers and depths, textures and tastes, folds of woman skin. He lay there and licked lightly with his tongue, not pursuing anything but what came next. He explored what she gave him, and wouldn't mind if the scarves were tighter, if he were held fast. He swallowed and felt her licking him and stopping. She would continue, he knew, absolutely, and he longed for more. The world became silent and solid flesh, a trustworthy place.

Scott had just kept talking, until he was in tears and not even angry. She tried to touch him. He shook his head, looking down like a child. This was what you got.

"I don't get you people," he said. "I don't understand women like you." And she put a hand to his smooth blond cheek.

"You understand, you must try to understand," she said. "I told you it wasn't possible. You know that's true." She didn't know what to say, she had to touch him, now worse than ever. She had to make things worse.

"Please, don't. I can't anymore. I'm so ashamed, so humiliated."

"No, now, no."

"I am foolish. I am a fool."

She could not help but find his tears erotic, looked at his

arms where the sleeves of his T-shirt ended, the little concavity between his pectoral muscles. She wanted to touch him one last time, ease his loneliness, ease hers. She had to make things worse. She put a hand on each shoulder, tried to lean him back against something—the couch. He tensed and resisted the push.

"No, please, Mina, it's bad for me, we can't. I won't. Give me some air."

She thought of it, that certainly this was mean. But she couldn't help it. She stopped pressing for a second. He didn't move, his head hung low. She inhaled, her breasts soft and just inches from his head. He just needed to lean forward.

"It's OK, Scott, it's OK." He shook his head. "Come here."

Afterward she left him, alone in his hotel room, stricken and spent from loving the wrong person. She thought that when she had finally ended it she would feel relief and liberation. She thought it would simplify her life. Why, then, did she feel so much worse, so much more confused and trapped as she walked home from the hotel, not noticing the sun setting, the splattered orange light—the garish, Mexican postcard sunset.

One Week from Leaving

David waited for his wife in the foyer of their small house.

David and Mina were surely going to have an argument. David was ready. Mina thought if it were in a movie, you would see it from his point of view. Mina walking in the front door, glancing at her watch. The watch would indicate lateness, and David, already in the foyer, standing, arms folded in front of chest, indicating lateness.

Mina said, "I'm sorry I'm late." You wouldn't see David's response, which would be assumed, in cinematic conventions of what silence indicates, to be a shrug. But in fact David didn't shrug. He watched Mina for a real-time second and a half. This made Mina sort of half smile at him. The absence of a corresponding reverse on David's reaction would change the point of view—the viewer would identify with Mina's imploring him for a response. If David didn't respond, the scene would be all sympathy for Mina. It must change to a two shot, or David must begin talking. Or better yet, alternating reverse angles on the two, as they spoke, so the viewer would simply read the dialogue naturalistically, as in life. But if the film instead used reverse angles on each one as the other spoke, the words would be altered by the imagery, be read as reactive and dual, all about listening and response and not seem natural at all. But that would be a foreign film, wouldn't it? This was a domestic drama, a situation comedy. David and Mina, after all, learned their visual grammar of how couples argue from TV more than movies. Something invisible and conventional. This is aided by David's having enclosed the space physically, trapping them in the foyer and in the conversation. The scene is lit from the living room lamp, unseen, the foyer full of afternoon shadows. Mina gestured toward the living room doorway, and David headed that way as well until he stopped her in between the two rooms, not actually in her way, but arresting her movement somehow. Perhaps to keep them in the frame of a static shot. The dialogue now, overlapping, more real than real.

"I'm sorry, I had to—" Mina said.

"You don't use your car anymore, do you? You won't drive." She tried to move to the living room, but David stood directly in front of her. She shook her head.

"You have a problem with driving."

"I have no problem with driving. I know how to drive."

"Your car problem is what I'm getting at here, Mina."

"I have no problem with cars. I am not against cars. I haven't been, yes, but it doesn't mean I won't. I mean, drive, my car, soon, at some point when I deem it necessary."

"Unless—" he said.

"Unless what? Unless driving has taken on some symbolic meaning for me? Unless not driving is my expression of dysfunction? Some deep-rooted ambivalence about my life, or some adolescent rebellion, some—"

"Or maybe you're scared to drive?" he said.

"It's not as if I've stopped bathing or something. You can't be committed for refusing to drive."

"Well, it certainly hasn't kept you at home. I mean, we can rule out agoraphobia, can't we?" They were still toe to toe in the doorway between foyer and living room. Perhaps a close-up of her eyes as they glanced from him to the room and back again.

Mina tried to smile at David.

"I'm starving. Let's get something to eat."

"OK, let's go out and eat. You drive us to a restaurant," David said, arms still folded. The challenge.

"No. I don't want to go to a restaurant. I work in a restaurant."

"Fine. Let's drive to the supermarket and buy food. Let's cook dinner."

"I'll give you a list."

"Look, I want to see you drive."

"David, I am so weary right now. Do we have to do this?"

"Do what?"

"OK, fine. Do you ever notice that when you drive the world becomes invisible?"

"No, I never noticed—"

"You're going places but you are not really moving, you're in the same place, the car? You play the radio, you look out the window, but you are not really in the world in any way?"

David now apparently felt the desire for some actorly activity. He left the doorjamb and entered the living room. He went to the liquor cabinet and opened it. Where did he learn this? Why fix a drink in the middle of an argument? It was more John Cassavetes than *The Thin Man*, but he hadn't seen any Cassavetes movies. He just wanted to be doing something. Mina lit a cigarette.

"Would you like a drink?" he asked.

"No, I have to go to work later."

He opened a bottle of wine and poured himself a glass. He also pulled out a cigarette. He patted his shirt pockets for a match (which was a terrifically cinematic thing to do, as he never had matches in his shirt pockets. In fact, he didn't even have shirt pockets—he was wearing a T-shirt, wasn't he?) while holding the cigarette in his mouth. She handed him her matches. He lit up.

"When you get where you are going," he said, exhaling, "you leave the car." He paused, looking down, thinking. " You are now in a new place. You walk when you get there. All it does is cut down the time in between where you started and where you are going. It is a simple device to enable you to move between places more quickly." He took another sip of his drink and leaned on the cabinet and he looked at his wife.

This would be the part where Mina would confess everything to David. In David's script of things she would have to start talking about why she lived for the in-between places, how she wanted the distance between things, why driving in this car-born place oppressed her. But then she would have to fill him in about Michael's cards and her affairs and her private obsessions and his best friend, Max, and her private shopping and her desperation. But of course she wouldn't. Because not all secrets can be told. He didn't really want to know. In a movie there would be a sense of narrative closure. In a script, revelation was liberating and solved everything.

This was not what was going to transpire between Mina and David.

She didn't want more liberation—she wanted something else. She'd not find out his secret life, or he, hers. And even if they tried, it could only be partial. They could exchange monologues for hours and it wouldn't reveal all. What would they have then—a catalog of unforgivable tabloidisms, an indelible ugliness. The equivalent of vomiting on each other. And even then, it was not really the full story. Some things would never be known. They could exhaust their secrets and they would still be discontinuous forever, static, however disclosed.

"You like to drive. I don't," she said.

Fourth Road Stop:
New Orleans

"Fashion is a form of daydreaming," Lorene said to me when we opened her first restaurant. I remember she was picking clothing for the opening, and we stood before her closet, stuffed with seven decades of clothing in size six. A few things were bigger or smaller, but so beautiful they were bought for their own sake, never to be worn, but just so they could hang in a closet and mean something about her. She was handing me a gift. I unwrapped the Japanese rice paper. I held a bone-cream silk nightgown. It was exactly that, a gown to be worn at night. The fabric was microthin, delicate, and yet so densely and finely woven it appeared to be a sheet of skin.

I watch Lorene sitting in the outdoor cafe in the French Quarter, waiting to meet me. She doesn't see me yet, but I am watching her wait.

I had draped the nightgown on her blond-wood dressing table and begun to undress. This was a gesture between women — undressing in front of each other, without embarrassment or comment. It was trusting them with your deepest secrets.

"It's a way of reimagining yourself. You wish upon a dress and a hue, and it's a prayer of transformation." I was naked in front of her three-way mirror and I let the nightgown slip down over my head. It did just that, slipped and slid over my body, a whisper of beige silk. The dressing room smelled of Shalimar perfume, the perfume of American women in the fifties who dreamed of exotic places, harems and veils, Louis Jordan European lovers, or Vittorio Gassman in Venice, making them wicked and undoing their dumb American naivete. The nightgown did not have lace trim, just delicate filigree-scalloped edges at the neckline and hem. The scallops flirted with skin and fabric, so the gown seemed to tease at what was silk and what was skin.

"How do you feel?" she asked.

"Like I should be climbing down a trellis covered in roses to meet my lover in the middle of the night. I'll catch the edges on thorns but it will be worth it."

"With a cool desert midnight breeze making you shiver slightly."

It is disconcerting to see Lorene sitting at a cafe in New Orleans waiting for me. It is the first time we have separated on our trip, and I am now finally able to look at her. She is wearing the same tight jeans she has worn since Texas and a black T-shirt. Her hair falls in her face, which is actually sun-kissed and golden brown. What sort of daydreaming did this indicate? If Lorene at nineteen was my first experience of the power of beauty and style—what had occurred? I am the same as I always am, in a thin cotton dress and sandals, hair hanging long down my back. A woman like Lorene can be read in the complicated ways she reinvents herself, in the way she appears.

I think of my father, sitting on the set of one of his films, talking to his assistant director, Dennis. I stood behind them, unseen (something that had became a habit), an invisible fourteen-year-old constantly lurking behind long hair and baggy clothing. They were seated, backs toward me.

"She's not a beauty like her mother," my father said. "But she has a good body, probably, long legs, and she'll have a kind of cheerleader charm."

"You sound disappointed," Dennis said. "At least she's not fat."

"No, no. Stop it. She is my daughter."

I already knew at fourteen that I was no genius like Michael, skidding through books and skipping grades with casual dash. And then, right then, I realized I would never be a great beauty either. I was consigned to the ordinary. And it was the beauty part I missed more. I didn't cry, I knew it was true. And the events that followed that conversation on the set were colored by this realization. A desire to be extraordinary in some way and not knowing how I could be.

I stand on the cobbled edge of the street and watch Lorene sipping her espresso. She is an epic beauty—someone could launch a war over her face, or even over the mere delicate poetry of her wrists and slender hands.

Finally I approach her. She looks up, ravishing and slightly grubby, the face now wearing a sun-crinkled smile—a smile to wash the world, I think.

I want to tell her about something true. I want her to understand and absolve me.

"Are you ready to leave?"

Lorene smiles at me and shakes her head. She pats the seat next to her. She sips her coffee and doesn't look at me.

"I don't think I'm going to New York with you, doll." I didn't expect her to say this.

"You're not?"

Lorene puts a hand on mine and squeezes.

"C'mon. I think I want to be here for a while. By myself. Stay away from hyper urban centers and old lovers. Unwind a bit. You go on and see your mom and your brother. I'll see you back in L.A."

"I just called my mother. Michael isn't even there yet."
Lorene says nothing. There is a woman at the next table, by
herself. I can see her over Lorene's shoulder. She's in a black
dress. She is wearing way too much makeup. One of those old
ladies who somehow has forgotten how to put lipstick on. They
run it outside the edges of their lips a bit until their mouth
looks punctured and sore. The makeup feathers in the vertical
wrinkles puckered around their lips. There is too much powder over it all. It cakes in corners. They get lipstick on their
teeth. They refuse to notice. Or maybe they don't care. But for
some reason they keep caking on the makeup, every day. She
is sipping a Coke through a straw. I can't stop watching her. Of
course she is smoking a cigarette.

"I'll leave in the morning. New Orleans depresses me, anyway."

Lorene nods.

"Hey, Lorene, do you remember my father's friend Dennis
Halpern," I say.

"Lean sycophant AD with penetrating sleazy gaze," she
says, not hesitating.

"Yeah. That's him."

"Yeah, I remember Dennis."

"He was the first guy."

Lorene gestures at the waiter for another coffee, for me.

"What?" she says. She's already forgotten our road project.

"I was fifteen, and we were having one of those long dinner
parties at the house. One of the last ones before Mom left. I
had a few glasses of wine through dinner and listened to
Michael and my father argue about politics. The party dis-
persed into little candlelit groups as usual. Some people went
to the pool and got high. Some people stayed at the dinner

table and talked. Others sat in the kitchen sipping wine and talking, putting away dishes and laughing occasionally. It was a jolly desert night, where the general feeling was warm and loose."

"I remember Michael talking about those dinner parties. Everyone envied your family. Your family actually had groupies, he said."

"I was not taken with any of these warm murmuring subgroups and went to my room to listen to my records and petulantly lie on my bed. Soon I started to touch myself in the way I did routinely then. I put my hands in my jeans and thought of, well, what girls think of at fifteen."

"What did you think of?" Lorene asks, allowing her sentence to rise at the end like a real question.

"That's not what this story is about," I say, smiling, blushing.

"Come on, I want to know," she says, laughing, putting her hand on my knee.

"I honestly don't remember. But, all right, for the sake of the story, let's say I was thinking about the handsome scarred Indian in *The Searchers*, the one who captures Natalie Wood."

"I remember him," and Lorene is really laughing now. "Captured by Indians, ooo—"

"All right, are you through? Let's move on here."

She smiles and nods. "You know what I used to think about when I was fifteen?" she says.

I look again past Lorene's shoulder at the woman at the next table. She's old, very old, and I watch her sip her Coke and move her lips. She's talking softly to herself. I watch for a second, to make sure, yes, very much murmuring to herself. Lorene is talking, talking.

"I used to think about Gram Parsons," she says. "Tragic cult rock star. Sweet, Southern-boy angel, a Christian junkie, in one of those cool Nudie suits he wore—you know, those suits with appliqué birds and marijuana flowers on them that Southern rocker boys used to get at Nudie's Western store in North Hollywood, back in the early seventies during that weird segue between hippies and glam rock."

I look at Lorene and shake my head. She thinks about clothes even when she masturbates.

"OK, Dennis," she says.

"Skip it."

"Come on, tell me. I'm listening."

"Christ, OK. I was in my room, by myself, hating the warm embrace of my family, wanting separateness. Then there was a low knock at my door. It's Dennis, with a drink and a joint, and he asks me if I want to get high. I'm rumpled and dizzy with dreams of erotic kidnappings. I let him in and we get stoned. He listens to my records with me and then he does the California come-on."

"He gives you a massage."

"Yes. And Lorene, to be touched felt so terrific. I leaned into it, and we were soon out of our clothes and on the floor of my room."

"With your whole family just down the hall."

"With my father's best buddy. It was done rather easily, and I sensed after it was done a kind of paleness in his face. I think he realized then that this was a pretty odd situation, somewhat combustible, to say the least. I was suddenly in a panic."

"It is important to get this right, the part afterward," Lorene says. She is right, it feels absolutely necessary to get it precisely correct. To articulate something, if it gets at all at the thing, if it makes some narrative cohesion of it, even if it is not the truth but the "truth," is the only way to escape the things that bind your life. It's the only way to make a life your life. The woman at the next table makes tiny gestures with her hands. She seems to think she's invisible, murmuring to herself, in public.

" 'What happens now?' I asked him.

" 'Nothing happens,' he said.

" 'But what about my father? We can't tell him.' Dennis was getting dressed and he looked hard at me.

" 'Of course we can't tell your father, Mina. It's a secret.' I, of course, started to cry at this point. He zipped his pants up. He said something to the effect of 'Why are you crying?' Then, I remember this, he said, 'Things like this happen every day.'

" 'Not to me,' I said. 'I don't know why I'm crying.' And I'll never forget what he said next.

" 'Look, Mina,' he said, 'let me let you in on a secret. Your father has a girlfriend. You know, his assistant Sheila?'

" 'He does not,' I said, really crying.

" 'Your father's sleeping with Sheila, his assistant. Or at least he was.'

" 'No, that can't be true,' I said.

" 'Yes. It's a secret. Everyone has secrets just like this one. Even your mother, believe me, has her secrets—' I stopped him, I guess, with my expression. But I knew it was true. He was right. The world, the grown-up world, was full of not-so-secret secrets. And really secret secrets. I thought of my uncles and aunts at family gatherings, and of distant looks at off-sides moments, unwrapping a present or pouring a drink. They were maybe thinking really of a secret life somewhere. Maybe even a grand passion. And it made them all seem complicated and sad in ways they hadn't before. They were wives and husbands, human and full of desire, and no one knows, or maybe everyone does. And sometimes it is that way forever, and sometimes things break down and dissolve. My mother left my father the following year. And I never told anyone—well, except Michael, and now you—about Dennis."

"All those stories are the same," Lorene says. "Anyway, finding out everyone is weak and human happens sooner or later, anyway. It just seems a shame we can't get any comfort out of knowing we are mostly all this way."

The old woman is definitely talking softly to herself. Maybe she is finally telling someone all the things she never said in her life. Her secrets, except now no one is left who cares. And it's unbearably lonely to have a secret that never gets told. It doesn't exhibit its secretness unless it is known. It is made to be violated. Or maybe not. Maybe the old woman's just crazy.

Mina could not stop thinking about Scott. She couldn't shake the awfulness of how he had looked at her. She couldn't shake the misery of Max's videos either, or another fight with David because he guiltily returned from some secret meeting with whomever he met and returned from. She headed to the Gentleman's Club, the night streets all cool desert and truly deserted.

Sex was not what worried Mina. It was everything else.

She for the first time felt a kind of queasiness about wanting Max. She felt the hangover of Scott, and it gave her the doom-laden bends thinking of how things had developed with Max. Of what possible outcome there would be, because affairs didn't just stay in one place. They didn't progress necessarily, but they went places. The more static you try and make them, the faster they slip into strange, unforeseen places.

At first it was how often. Once a week only. Between one

and four. This was not negotiable. Max, despite his gut and his smoking and his paper-strewn house, adhered to rather strict rule making. The more arbitrary, the more vehemently he clung to it. Mina had to meet him once a week, but on constantly changing days. Monday this week, Tuesday the next, Wednesday the next. No discernible patterns must evolve, he said. But then it became impossible. They took more chances, they saw each other more often, she just had to. But the more they saw each other, the more elaborate the paranoia and the more complicated the restrictions became. He freely engaged, enthusiastically engaged, in the particularly dangerous and impractical liaison with his best friend's wife. And yet he displayed rigid logic and rationalism in his execution of the affair, as if these rules mitigated it somehow, made it tolerable. The way he made her take a shower before she left. She knew then she would become a lightning rod for a subrational guilt. An intolerable transgression that fueled an excessive passion. And a hypervigilance, seen only in the most haunted men, combat vets, murderers, executioners, sweaty embezzlers, and Max. How is it she came to feel sorry for him? How is it she found his paranoia erotic, and she never felt guilt, she just didn't think about it? So it was not really as odd as it might have seemed, given these rules, when they actually stopped having sex. Or intercourse, rather. Max liked to videotape her before, get her undressing, ask her questions. They both found this erotic. Then yesterday it finally happened. He asked her to lie on the bed. He continued videotaping. He instructed, and she obeyed. You look sexy, he said. And she knew instantly where it was going, but she played dumb. Because sex was a sort of anagram for them, a way of merely organizing and reordering the same elements. First I do this and then you do that. Say this while I do that. The next time, he goes first. There were just so many possible combinations and variations. So she absolutely knew that the camera would become the preeminent thing between them, the variable that multiplied the limited possibilities. Show me what you do by yourself, he said. He was still taping. She didn't care. She put her hand under her panties. No, don't close your eyes, he said. And she opened them. Open your legs, he said. He sat in the chair, fully dressed.

"You like this?" he asked.

"Yes," she said.

"Mina, I can't see what you're doing."

"I know. But I do it like this. With the panties on."

He smiled behind the camera.

"OK, but today I want you to take off your panties."

"You come here and take them off," she said.

"No."

"Put down the camera and come here."

"No, now just do what I say."

Mina pulled her underwear down. She started to touch her pubic hair. She would be able to come quickly. She knew how easy it would be, she found a sideways angle on her clitoris, pushing her index finger fast against it. She looked at the reflection in the lens, her lover behind it. He moved toward the bed, still filming. He put his hand on her knee and pushed her thighs apart.

"I can't with them apart," she said.

"You can do it. Come on, I want to see better."

"I can't."

"You can do it. You'll like it. I want to see."

Mina came, and her legs shook, and the difficulty of it made it more intense.

"Come here now. I want you to come here now."

Max kept taping.

"It's late. You should go."

"Please, Max."

"It's late."

Later, at the restaurant he had called her. He told her he was watching her video. That he was very close to coming. And as the servers and customers crowded by her, she listened to him come. It was then she knew that it was going to be like this now, his way with her. She was, she had to admit, excited by it, this new place.

www.missingchildren.com

Lisa logged on to Mark's computer while the twins slept in the next room. The blue light of the computer in a dark room made her hungry. She ate a chocolate bar and followed her anxiety to pixels and abstracted places. A warning was issued in a box: *Any information you submit is insecure and could be observed by a third party in transit.*

No button worked unless she pressed the OK button. It didn't give you the option of "yes," but just a resigned "OK." The other options were to "cancel" or "do not warn again," which was like a permanent OK. She clicked on "OK," agreed to the terms, to third-party observations. She appreciated the warning—now she was out there and in the open road. She first was shown tips to avoid abduction.

Teach your children to be wary of strangers.

Then she was shown the phone number for information: 1-800-MISSING. It was a ghoulish thing, this combination of technology and tragedy. She pressed on to the search for faces. This was the directory she had compiled in her mind every day. First the words came. Numbers and names. Dates of birth. Dates last seen. And a phrase categorizing the crimes:

> *Endangered Missing*
> *Lost Injured Missing*
> *Family Abduction*
> *Endangered Runaway*

That was all. Whole stories and whole lives shorn of all but these categories. Abduction, endangered. Certainly. Missing. And then after the numbers and the facts came the faces, straining across some cyberspace, one appearing before another, some taking longer and partially appearing and then slowly coming into focus. The page now had faces next to numbers, some in black-and-white and some in color. They were four years old and smiling in a class photo, or black-and-white and at a distance. They were twelve and already more reserved, or seventeen and far away. They were nine and with those oversized adult teeth, and Lisa could not stop scrolling and examining all their faces, already familiar and not so distant from the twins, already lost forever to their families, and the faint hope of this place.

Someone stirred in the room. She turned and her son was there, in his foot pajamas and his half-asleep face. His hand rubbed his eyes as he watched her, backlit by the screen of the computer with all the faces of the lost.

"Alex, baby, why are you out of bed?" she asked, turning, blocking the screen from view.

"I had a nightmare, Mom," he said, his voice teetering on crying, the very vocalizing of the word *nightmare* frightening him into tears. She went to him and knelt beside him. Lisa picked her son up into her arms and held him. He sighed into her shoulder and she rocked him, just like when he was a tiny baby, she swayed in the familiar rhythm of babies and mothers, something that was slipping away as they grew older, something that every day soothed a little less as he got bigger. They were gradually losing their perfect rhythm of two, except for moments like these when the night scared him back into her arms. It worked, he relaxed and it was better, it was perfect and he could stop crying. Lisa put him on his bed by his sleeping sister, and she watched them both as they slept.

In the other room the computer said "Good-bye" in a strangely chipper voice and disconnected. From lack of activity. She sat, but she was not still. She sat, vigilant and listening, deep into the night.

"Ms. Delano?"

"Yes. Who is this?"

"This is your father's friend, Bill."

"Oh, yes. Bill. Bill Collector. I remember you. What's up?"

"I need to get in touch with your father, Jack Delano."

"Well, that is touching, Bill. But I don't know how to reach him."

"I'll just keep calling, Ms. Delano."

Pause.

"You will, won't you. You really are a sweetheart, aren't you? The sum of twenty-one centuries of human striving. The zenith of contemporary culture, the Enlightenment realized, the dreams of Thomas Jefferson fulfilled. Nietzsche's *Übermensch*. John Ford's quiet man. Your mother must be very proud."

"Ms. Delano. Your father has no honor."

"You don't know about my father, you hopeless little sleaze-ball. Clearly you know nothing about honor. What kind of man are you? A real man would rather beg on the streets than call strangers and harass them about debts their parents supposedly owe and threaten and you dare even use a word like honor. You have no shame, Bill."

Click.

Ring. Ring. Ring.

"Hello."

"You shouldn't hang up on me, Ms. Delano. It's very rude. Don't make me take measures . . . of a legal nature. Just tell me where your father can be reached."

"Look, Bill, I'm going to level with you, all right?"

"Please."

"My father is dead, OK? He had a tragic beach accident. It's really very painful. I'd rather not discuss it at this point. So you can put his card in the expired file. Just tear it up."

"Ms. Delano?"

"Yo."

"I can't do that, you know. You could right his debts, you know. We could work out a payment plan. You could do it for your father's memory. Get rid of these calls forever by paying his debt."

"I don't care, Bill. You can call me for the rest of your life. I can be your life's obsession, if you like. Take my number home and put it under your pillow so you can call me early in the morning. I'll give you my work numbers so you can call me there. I'll give you my lovers' numbers, both of them, so you know where to reach me in the afternoon. I'll be your life's work, if you like. Go ahead. I like the attention."

THE LAST VIDEO

Audio: Muffled.

MINA

What are you doing?

Image appears, just shadow.

MAX (O.S.)

I'm turning on the camera.

MINA

Oh.

MAX (O.S.)

Turn on the lamp by the night table.

We hear a click and the room is low lit by the table lamp. Midshot of GIRL on the bed, the sheet pulled up around her breasts, smoking a cigarette. The bedroom is disordered, clothes strewn everywhere, books, ashtrays full of cigarettes, an open bottle of wine and half-finished glasses.

MAX (O.S.)

Why don't you take the lamp shade off? I'm not
getting enough light.

She does this. She just casually bats the shade off. She looks at
the camera, smoking. The naked lightbulb lights her from
down up, casting backward shadows on her cheeks and brow.

MAX (O.S.)

You look like night of the living dead.
Zombielike. But a sexy zombie.

GIRL smiles at the camera.

MAX (O.S.)

It's the naked bulb. The cigarette. Your slightly
dirty smile. Tabloid, like those Hollywood
Babylon police photos. Starlet found murdered
in bed.

MINA

Black Dahlia. Fatty Arbuckle. Errol Flynn.

MAX (O.S.)

Bloodstained sheets and empty whisky bottles.
She's clutching the suicide note in her white
fist.

MINA

Clara Bow. Lana Turner. Sal Mineo. Lupe
Valez. Virginia Rappe.

                    MAX (O.S.)
Uremic poisoning. Yes, that's the feel. That's the
general ambience.

                    MINA
But it's just a no-name girl. A quiet, simple,
everyday infidelity, your bad lighting and your
messy apartment. You provided the sordid frame.

                    MAX (O.S.)
But it suits you. Squalor and dirty sheets and a
solitary moment on camera. You look sexy.

GIRL exhales and reaches over to extinguish her cigarette. The
sheet falls from her breasts and she lets it bunch by her waist.
She looks at the camera.

                    MINA
Max—

                    MAX (O.S.)
No talking. Just sit there.

                    MINA
Max, I think I'm not into where this is going.
Seriously.

                    MAX (O.S.)
Shh. I don't want talking. Just be quiet. This time
quiet. Girl, in bed, no-name girl. This is
postcoital. This is the tryst at its most signifying

moment. There is the smell, slight but there too, of sex. The camera gets this somehow, too. Maybe removing the light shade is to compensate for not being able to have the smell on camera.

MINA

It's a bit cliché, don't you think? It's not very interesting. Besides, there is no coital anymore, is there? Not post or pre. We are perpetually faux coital.

MAX (O.S.)

Don't spoil things, Mina.

MINA

Spoil things? In case you haven't noticed, I don't like this video shit anymore.

MAX (O.S.)

Let's not have an Edward Albee moment, shall we? And it's not videotape. It's digital, by the way.

MINA

Jesus. The thing is, I'm really bored. Really. Don't look so surprised. Besides, I thought you found the truth so fucking fascinating.

There is a long pause.

MAX (O.S.)

What's fascinating to me right now is your silence and my filming it here on this bed with

the dirty-cliché sheets and the smell-evoking
Hollywood-scandal lightbulb.

GIRL shrugs and puts out her cigarette. She waves him off and
gets up from the bed. She starts to get dressed.

MAX (O.S.)

What interests me is that dirty smile on your
face. The utter lack of regret or even a vague
sadness. No thought of your young husband
waiting at home. No thought of climbing into
bed with him when your long blond hairs are
still mussed from my sheets. And not just
anyone, no, but David, young kind trusting
David, has not only had his wife sleep out, but
she's chosen his oldest and best friend to fuck.
In one act his life is transformed into the
tritest, most distasteful display. And he doesn't
even know it. Humiliations visited beyond his
belief.

GIRL purses her lips. She listens, but continues dressing.

MAX (O.S.)

And there you are, unembarrassed. Unashamed.
You think, Well, it's you too, Max. You are his
best friend. But we know I'm a bastard. We
know no sordid situation is too much for me.
We know how I crave aberrance. It's in my
makeup, isn't it? That's why you want me. I
would never have talked you out of it. I would

solicit it. That's what you desire in me. You were
so bored and frustrated with your own stupid
life, you can only be turned on by humiliation
and aberrance. His best friend. That's why you
like the dirty sheets and the naked lightbulb.
That's what you're here for.

GIRL is now dressed. She grabs her purse, glances at the camera.
The camera pulls in to a CLOSER SHOT. She shakes her head.

> **MAX (O.S.)**

Mina.

GIRL shakes her head and turns away. She heads to the door.

> **MAX (O.S.)**
> You're not leaving, are you?

Another long pause. GIRL is putting on her earrings.

> **MAX (O.S.)**
> Mina? Don't leave, c'mon.

> **MINA**

I am leaving now.

The camera stays on GIRL. We hear MAX breathe off camera.
She is about to leave and then she goes back, reaches over to
the lamp, and clicks it off.

TITLE: END

*   *   *

It was the three of them again—on the porch. Max sat at David's feet, and Mina was thinking, I want to kill Max for having it over on David. It was a slow pulse, it was in how he inhaled his cigarette. It was how he ate his chips. It was the subtext of his conversation. I fucked your wife. It occurred to Mina, the lousy and far-reaching meanness of what Max and she did. She thought, Christ, he really must never know. No matter what happened. She swore if Max gave her one goddamned look, one "special" smile . . . But no. He sat there, laughing and talking as usual. He had no heart. Or he hid it well.

"So watch this," David said. He threw a bottle cap across the porch. It bounced once, then landed on the wood molding, where it stopped, perched.

"Impressive," Max said, and chucked a bottle cap in the same direction. It hit the porch floor, then skidded off to the side. No bounce.

"Shit," Max said. David took another bottle cap and threw it. It bounced perfectly, and followed the trajectory of the first, coming to a stop on the wood molding.

"Shit, David." Max picked up another and got ready to throw it.

"Turn it sideways as you throw," David said.

"OK, now I see," Max said. He bounced it. This time it got a bounce but missed the ledge. "OK, all right, now I'm almost there."

David threw. It did precisely what the first one did. Max threw. It was off but closer. David threw. Max. David. Mina sipped her beer. She watched them.

"So, this is your afternoon writing distraction," Max said, aiming. David laughed.

"You figured it out. What about your work?"

"I've got some crappy trailers I've been writing to make a few bucks. No time for anything else."

"What about that girl from Taylor's?" David asked.

"The barista," Max said.

"Yes, the barista," David said. They both said it annoyingly, as if it were a strongly accented Spanish word. *Bareeesta*. The *bareeeesta*.

"Well, the barista is not likely to make a second showing," Max said.

David hucked one more bottle cap. He missed this time, actually.

"Really, why is that?" David asked. Max grinned closed-mouthed.

"Well, she got offended by something I did. Or didn't do, I guess."

"What?" David asked, smiling, "What happened?"

"Well, nothing. I just spent some time with her, and then I had to leave right after it was over because it was late . . ."

"Oh, no. Right after?" David asked.

"Well, after I washed off in the bathroom. Yeah, pretty much right after. I could tell she was irritated. When she saw I was getting ready to go, she started to say, rather nastily, I might add, 'Just go. OK, I have to get up. Please hurry.' That kind of thing. I felt bad, but I was tired and I didn't want to be there. It's lousy, I know."

"The old dine and dash," David said.

"Fuck and flight," Max said.

"Suck and scram," David said, now laughing.

"Rut and run."

"Lick and leave."

"Poke and peel."

"Bang and banish."

"Bang and banish? Jesus, David, banish?" And Max started laughing. David laughed so hard his chest started to shake. Max now couldn't stop. Mina watched them laughing and she decided she hated Max. Never again would he touch her, the bastard. Or watch her, really, or film her, for God's sake. She got up and abruptly exited the porch, heading into the house. She heard the screen door slam behind her. She could hear them from the porch.

"What's with Mina?" from Max.

"Oh, nothing. She's acting sensitive. She knows we're just joking. You know Mina."

"Yeah."

"Come on, Meenee," David shouted. "Come back out. Come on."

"Come on, Mina," Max said.

"Oh, Mina Mina," David said.

"MinaMina," Max echoed. They both said it like it was one name—Minamina. And then mimiced each other and giggled.

"Minamina."

Bastards.

"Hey, is she still not driving?" Max said, his voice low but still audible.

"I guess not."

"I think I got it, look," Max said, and then the sound of the bottle cap bouncing. Mina stayed in the house until Max left. Later she emerged and opened the door to David's office. The blue-green glow met her.

"What's this, David?" Mina saw on David's computer what looked remarkably like Max's front stoop, in video grainy surveillance black-and-white. She looked at the address at the top of the monitor: *www.espialvid.com*.

David was in the kitchen.

"Oh, that's a surveillance site. One of about ten thousand. This one shows movies made out of security tapes. Some even have narratives." He came out of the kitchen with a beer. He looked at the screen. A woman with her face digitally altered so the features were blurred beyond recognition was entering and then leaving the house. It went on and on; sometimes she looked at the camera and sort of waved before she was let in. Mina, of course, recognized herself. She felt herself flush as she watched. She was not able to breathe for a moment.

"What's interesting here is that the usual thing about surveillance is the subject not knowing he or she is being filmed. We get that voyeur vulnerability thing. But this is a security camera that she knows is there. See, she waves at it sometimes. But she doesn't know it has been edited and recorded and pieced together. So her knowing she is being filmed is subverted by her being made into a story of sorts. A narrative compiled without her knowing, by someone unseen. Apparently a person she knows well and trusts. But here she is on the Internet, and you sense she must not know because the face is blurred to protect her privacy. Or a better way of putting it is her face is blurred so it can be used to violate her privacy."

Mina stared at herself, unidentifiable in the poor resolution of the tape. She looked at David. He didn't recognize her, he really didn't.

"Or maybe it's all an affectation and she does know, and the digital altering is just to create a violating effect. She could be an actress, but these surveillance sites are supposed to be strictly for the unknowing subject. Other sites have knowing subjects. Kind of exhibition stuff. Not nearly as pornographic as this stuff. It's mesmerizing, isn't it."

Mina felt her life kaleidoscoping into something else, something she knew nothing about. She thought about all the videotapes Max took. The ones she knew about and the ones she didn't.

"Turn it off, David. It's horrible. Turn it off."

She walked to the Gentleman's Club to get drunk. Maybe Lorene was still there. She should not be surprised. She should have seen this coming. She walked fast, not feeling gravel or sidewalk.

The thing was that it no longer mattered. It was over. But it disturbed her. All that mattered was his filming her, and she had just begun to understand this. Mina had just begun to locate her need to be filmed. Located it as a female affliction, even. She had always had the sneaking feeling that she was being filmed. She felt she was being watched at all times. It was sort of like believing God watched, except Mina didn't believe in God. But she did believe someone was paying attention. That if you lined up the narrative of her life, the secret triumphs and humiliations, that it had a coherence, that she in some way made a kind of sense, that who she was now and what she did now were completely understandable, even sort of engaging, if viewed in the context of every possible minute that led up to it. Perhaps this was a sort of milky modern morality, that you were being paid attention to, or that you should put on a good show, one full of moving and sympathetic characters.

Mina imagined this might be a particularly female perception. That women were in a way programmed to be animated by the attention of others. What Lorene said, the other day: we don't exist if people don't pay attention to us. Of course it wasn't true, but it felt true. And this was irrational, but it explained why being filmed by Max was so deeply erotic. That it seemed to deeply reveal her inner self, the part of her that felt perpetually animated by the gaze of others. She had felt something irrational and pathetic, and this made it legitimate and real. She was being watched, she wasn't crazy or deluded after all. And it wasn't about vanity, damn it, it was about having the feeling that your life was being attended, about having your life signify something, some true thing. And that's why it gratified her — being filmed was familiar and comforting from the first moment. Even Max didn't realize this. She pretended otherwise. Why did Max want so badly to film her? Now, that's the question. Because the gazer must certainly want something, too.

Sex was never the problem. It was, in fact, the only possible real thing in her life. The way it took the rule of two and made a mess of it, destroying and exhausting. There was nothing that couldn't be brought to sex or found in it, and it made all the conversation dumb. But this was not a world where sex was understood. In all her life she could not imagine, no matter what, not wanting sex, would always hope for its transformations, its undoing alchemies. It was finally her only answer to her family, the only thing the world had to match the loss of her family, the loss of innocence, the only compensation for having to grow up and grow old. The only thing not given in her family was sex, so it made a perverse kind of sense that families were born of sex. The cold reality of sex, the way it made you bodied and exposed to someone not you, my God, the reveling in the body, the hushed words that flew, the desperate feelings. And yes, even in the most rote situation of it, even in its awkward moments when you thought banally—too long, lower, almost—even, or especially, then, the ordinary things of bodies. Her wounds exposed, and then she is embraced, or embraces, and she looks at him (it could be any one of them) and they are human and male and flawed, so fragile, but so different, such a strangeness to behold. And this was the pleasure she knew, the secret heart of all people, to be loved like this, perpetually strange, the bravery in it, the complications.

She sat at the bar at the Gentleman's Club and waited for Lorene to close up. Mina thought maybe the thing to do was to have children. Maybe that's the thing to make sex stick. If that could make the bodily need of difference and strangeness become the undying connection of the ultimate familiar thing—a body born of you—a family.

"Can I get you something?" Ray asked.

"Liquid Oblivion. With ice."

He started in with the club soda.

"Ray, a real one. Whatever cheap pour."

He didn't even look up and poured her a glass of caramel-brown liquid.

"In movies in the forties, when you ordered a drink in a bar, the bartender would place a shot glass in front of you and then put the bottle next to it, letting the orderer pour the drink himself. It's almost a testament to seriousness. A certainty that one will not be enough. Leave the bottle. Pretend I'm John Garfield. That's right. Thank you."

Mina downed the drink, took the bottle and poured another.

Lorene wore gray silk trousers and a cashmere sweater, also pearl gray. She watched Mina.

"Sit down. It's rude to make a lady drink alone."

Lorene sat next to her on a bar stool. Ray placed a glass in front of her and Mina poured her a drink.

"I hadn't noticed any ladies drinking," she said. Mina smiled.

"You're cute, doll," Mina said, nodding at the glass.

Lorene drank it in one shot. They sat quietly for a while.

"All right, you're upset."

Mina nodded. "Your razor-accurate perception again in evidence. How do you do it, Lorene?"

"So you're angry at me?"

"What about sex. I mean, you apparently never have it, don't need it, do you?"

"You are having enough sex for both of us."

"It's the only thing I like. I like sex. I love sex."

"You know, it's impossible to have sex with everyone. You have to limit it or it doesn't mean anything. It's a triage kind of thing—you have a limited capacity and have to be selective in where it is applied."

They sat quietly as the restaurant closed down around them. Mina looked at Lorene in the semidark. She put her hand on Lorene's wrist. Lorene held her hand as they sat.

Mina shook her head. Lorene drank another shot. So did Mina.

"You don't even know the half of it."

"Well, I know more than you think. It's not all that difficult to figure out."

"It's funny, Lorene, that men are called callous for wanting to sleep with different women."

"You've been thinking about that."

"Yes, I have. They are called inconstant and callow. They

fear depth. But what is it that makes men long for different women, if not desire for a different soul, if not attention to the ways each woman is different from all the others. In truth, I love the longing of men, the dire way they want all women, and I've felt it myself. I could fall for anyone, find all their calamitous, ridden selves deathly appealing at the right moment."

"In the right light."

"It's not necessarily something I want to be cured of—desire."

Lorene got up from her bar stool. She started to shut off the lights and pulled out her keys to lock up.

"All right, then there's no problem. So why are you sitting here in the dark?"

Mina leaned back against the bar, regarding her crossed legs. Lorene leaned over the bar and replaced the bottle.

"There are so many alternate fictions at work in my life right now."

"Lies, I believe, is the common name."

"Right, then, secrets, lies, fictions. Logistics. It's all about the mess of explanations and not the mess of bodies and souls. Lorene, I'm going in for the big car wreck, I'm heading—"

"Right. Well, and it would be the best thing to—"

"Right, run away—"

"Exit before it all collapses—"

"But."

"Look, maybe that's the intention all along. Maybe the desire is to mess it up until you have to leave, because that's really what you want all along." Lorene leaned toward her over the bar. "I decided the other day as I sat home, unable to leave the house, that I would go. So we'll go, we'll go together."

Mina shook off Lorene's suggestion of a lift home. She wanted a late-night, dangerous walk, a two-in-the-morning solitary walk home. Or maybe she wanted to pretend she was John Garfield for a little while longer.

David was asleep when she got there. She wanted to slip into bed next to him and rouse him slowly with kisses and caresses. But it would just be a fight about lateness and another round of edging toward explanations. Which was a shame, because she wouldn't mind holding him close right then, she was still certain that would make things better. Because tomorrow she would be leaving.

Her father had said to her once, I'm addicted to desire. That was before. Back when he had everything.

She constantly eavesdropped on him, or was inadvertent witness to a thousand of his indiscretions. Did he think she had no ears, no eyes? But she lurked, from lap to lap sleepily after dinner, playing with reading glasses in breast pockets and teaspoons on lemon twists and napkin rings. She experimented with drops of wine on sugar cubes. If she stayed quiet, often he let her stay for hours, head resting on the shoulders of a dozen eager "uncles" and "aunts." Many hands wanted to hold her, and she heard the murmur of adult voices as the sweetness of drifting in and out of wakefulness in candlelight surrounded her. It was always a special occasion, and he was not one to protect children. It was only later in her sulk of fourteen-year-old languor that explanations were offered. "Sara is my special friend, be nice to her," he would say, and she would shrug, unsmiling. He handed her his wallet. "Go get yourself something." She carried it with two hands in front of her. She wandered to a corner to look inside. Bills and bills. She bought so many things. She thought he'd ask, but he didn't. He just put the wallet in his pocket without even looking at the money left. Her mother bought in bulk and at thrift stores. She would say, Let's go to the bargain matinee. Mina took to pulling bills from his wallet whenever she could. Early in the morning, she slid stocking-footed into his sleep room and pulled a twenty or a ten. He never said a word, never a word.

It was an instant, really, a flash she looked at as the end of her childhood, or at least a precipice of her ending childhood from which she could see the terror and power of adulthood. Despite her father's explicit desire that she not associate with the "below the line" technical employees on the set, she found the makeup trailer the only hospitable hangout. She sat and watched them work, and out of boredom they would beckon her to the chair and start to play. One inspired afternoon, Jay, huge, bulk-muscled, and lavishly gay, cooed and applied artful pats of makeup to her young face. Emmy, who despite her dyed black crew-cut adored creating the most conventional beauty, fussed at her hair. And she loved it, being touched by more than one person at once, being touched at all—lately, it seemed people hesitated to touch her as much, especially her father, who nearly cringed when she leaned on his lap one night, so tired she'd forgotten her sulkiness and tried to settle in between his spread knees, perching on a thigh, head to chest, where she could survey the world from the smell of his soapy sweater. She felt a brittleness in his body, a reluctance, and she quickly untangled herself and went to lie in his trailer, wrapping a blanket as tightly around her body as possible. It was not so only with Michael, who would still wrestle and roughhouse as always, still throw an arm over her shoulder, still squeeze her head to his mouth and make smacking noises as he kissed. Even much later, when his episodes had apparently already begun, she took his arm and clung to him, satisfied that people might think he was her boyfriend, and he must have known, because he held open doors and lit cigarettes for her and bought her a rose from a ragged woman on the street.

Her father had no affection for her adolescence, and as the makeup and hair were played, she realized this was the most touching she had had all summer. She missed her mother so badly thinking of her own loneliness, she actually started to cry, only quickly stopping to prevent streaking her made-up face.

"You have the most beautiful skin," Jay said.

"Such soft hair," Emmy said.

"Wait until you see this," and she held still as he used small wet cold brushes that felt like a tiny tongue on her eyelid. It made her shudder. Jay smiled at her.

"Edie Sedgwick or Audrey Hepburn?"

"Rita Hayworth," she said, and they laughed at her, and powdered her and turned her finally to look in the mirror, and there she was, pixie woman-sex-child, and she could not stop staring, so mysterious she seemed. It was a heavy movie star look, but an accent here and a smoothness there and a slight artifice about the eyes that gave her a deliberate sexiness made her suddenly dangerous. "Wow," she said, and it changed the way she moved. She wandered about the set staring at people, anxious to be seen. It was this enjoyment of attention that worried her later when the incident with Dennis happened, and in her mind the makeup day and the incident were conflated, though she was aware that they very well might have occurred months apart, but memory had conflated them to make a logical narrative, to make a causal relation in which she could find some coherence. She felt the strain of trying to remember things as they actually were, the precise chronology, but it was hopeless, gone in a veil of wishes and regrets. How particularly when someone was ill, like her brother, the chain of your memories of that person alters irrevocably. His illness became like her own personal Hays office, erasing the offense and the disquiet from all her brother memories. There were, however, the seams of the edits, the wafting hints of darkness she had forgotten. How this kind of remembering was like insanity, and the way later disturbances threw off all the pleasant dreams of her brother. They must be there, the indications, the evidence. And so she would remember things, incidents to make the present presentable and understandable. She knew the incident with Dennis was colored like the memories of her father and her brother, it was colored by her no longer being able to believe in her own innocence, or any innocence at all, even though she also knew that reality was much more complex than innocence and culpability, cause and effect, truth and lies.

Road Stop: New Orleans

I wake in the hotel room. Lorene is out. Sitting in some cafe, no doubt, transforming into some kind of voodoo priestess. She doesn't want to leave. She says she wants to be in a place that respects decay. I still have to go to my mother's. I can't sleep. I watch TV.

John Ireland is in a gray-checkered suit, talking in a journalist weary sexy voice.

"Now you have a secret, too" is what Dennis had said.

But I didn't want a secret.

It was not Thanksgiving, but the week after. My body confirmed what I suspected all along: it was against me, an enemy. It was not pliant, it wanted things, it grew things.

Dennis had touched me because I had wanted him, too. I made him. He hesitated and I pushed him.

You could just undress like you did before. If you want.

Oh, I want, all right.

It wasn't Thanksgiving, but the week after.

He looked at me, OK? And no one seemed to see me at all. I felt for the first time electric and possible.

"She'll never be the beauty her mother was," my father had said.

"Everyone has secrets, people aren't what they seem."

"It's a surveillance site. For videotapes."

I felt my beauty upon me when men looked at me, it radiated out, electric, and illuminated the world.

My body had been doing strange things. Unfamiliar things.

"Your father," he said, "your mother."

You can count on it. You absolutely can.

John Ireland was married to Joanne Dru. In real life. I know this.

Every desire contains its counterdesire. It's already there, embedded.

How did—David had bruises on his hand.

He said, with absolute confidence, "You'll get over this."

It wasn't Thanksgiving, but the week after.

I wanted to get the thing over with, get it out of my body. Michael came home, to be there, the week after Thanksgiving. Left school and came home to me. Just like that.

He zipped up his pants. He didn't look at me in the same way.

Scott cried. It wasn't a movie to him, was it?

Michael took me to the clinic. They wouldn't let you do it unless you had someone to drive you home.

"What's up?" Michael said. "I hear this rumor you don't eat or speak anymore."

"No comment," I said.

When you ignore me I feel as though I don't exist.

"Just sit tight. I'll be there tonight."

"No, no, no," I said. But he came anyway. Took me to the clinic and drove me home. He put me to bed.

Lied to the doctor about being eighteen.

"You'll get over it," the doctor said. I didn't cry.

"Well?" Michael had asked, holding my hand while I lay in bed. I was groggy. What did I say to him?

"It's obvious, isn't it? I've ruined my life."

He said, Michael said, he looked at me and I remember what he said, "Nothing lasts, it doesn't. I promise."

"Is that a comfort or a threat?"

"The world is full of second and third and fourth chances."

"What?" I said.

"Go to sleep," he said. "I'll take care of you."

'What?" I said.

"Go to sleep."

"You've changed, Michael, I hate it."

"Yeah? I haven't. You're just getting older. You're just growing up. You're the one who's changed."

John Ireland's voice. It reminds me of my father.

The Morning of the Day They Leave

Lisa is cleaning Lorene's house when Lorene makes her an offer. She shows Lisa her alarm system. She gives her space in the closet. They set up the guest room for the twins. Lorene feels exuberant doing this, letting Lisa stay in her house. She was going to be gone for a month or so, and maybe by then Lisa's husband will have come back. Anyway, Lisa would enjoy it more than she did.

When Mina woke on her last day, she spent a minute staring at her husband. It was not even six o'clock. She couldn't wake him. It was overly dramatic to leave him a note. Besides, she didn't want to explain anything. She was so weary of trying to explain things. She sensed vaguely that she might regret that, and she started to walk to Lorene's apartment.

The walk up Franklin facing the Hollywood Hills was eerie and quiet this early. There were hot, dry blasts of wind, the late-summer Santa Anas that made the city feel strange. Hot paradoxical winds—winds that made you sweat. Mina felt the sirocco blast of air, an undercurrent of desert. Perfect weather for an exit. The air felt heavy and pushy, hot, sudden northern blows that Raymond Chandler called red winds. Well, he ought to know, and it felt that way, red and hot and skewed, as if it might blow the pages of a calender back, the introduction of a flashback, an incantation to time slips. Mina stood at Hollywood and Franklin and looked back down, listening to tiny pieces of paper swirling in the street. The dawn light deflected and diffused, a fighting orange, a growing umbery red. The wind was red because you could feel the tabloid bloodrush of the city in it, a cracked Southern California creepiness that came from desert and sun and all its golden promise. You could feel Manson at the edges, and fires and riots combusting from within, and the funny way the city always seemed primed for retribution.

Mina walked on, regarding the mock paradise. Sure, verbena and maidenhair and palm fronds, but, hey, also a Lysol alley starlet with a venereal disease, a serial killer with a keen sense of irony, a movie actor twitching on the ground while everyone watched, and the ghoulish glee of teenagers getting stoned at the alley where Sal Mineo was stabbed, or at Marilyn's crypt. There was no cliché that this place wearied of, nothing so shopworn and spent that it couldn't be revived with the right recasting, the right lighting, and the right framing.

What a great city, Mina thought, and for a moment she didn't want to leave, felt a kind of longing for it already.

Road Stop:
New York

I am sitting at my mother's kitchen table. The night before, when I arrived, my mother told me Michael had never shown up. Why does this not surprise me? We are looking at the little garden behind her building, Seventy-third Street behind us. It is one of those New York mornings, the *Times* and the coffee and the toasted bagels. My mother is quiet. I feel my life as sordid and almost ridiculous. What have you been up to? she asks me, and I have nothing to say. I am thinking of our family. My father in Ojai, just trying to live down his mistakes. I imagine he is at the Krotona library, or meditating on the sunset, or cooking his food for dinner. It isn't horrible. He seems not so bad from a distance.

"If Jack were a stranger, and I met him tomorrow, I might think he was kind of a cool guy, leaving his Hollywood life behind. I mean, dropping out so completely and just trying for some ordinary spiritual, whatever, transcendence."

"Your brother and your father are mysteries to me," she says.

"Michael, I thought I was coming here to save Michael. To finally make it up to him for making him a walking elegy to all my expectations. "

"I think it was always hard for you to accept him as he was, or as he is, I should say. But it wouldn't have made any difference. Nothing would have turned out any differently. I tried a million times to help Michael. It doesn't make any difference."

"Yeah, that's what you think."

"It's true. Some things are just unfixable, unanswerable."

"Well, I'm from fucking California and I want a goddamn answer."

My mother stops sipping her coffee. Then she smiles.

"Right."

My mother unscrews the top of a jar of jelly. She spreads some on her toast. I really like seeing this, my mother putting jelly on her toast. I feel as though I might cry, I'm just so happy watching her eat toast. I imagine David, waking alone and making his breakfast in our house. Isn't it funny how the people so familar to you, so close to you can seem impossible to grasp? You have to imagine them as strangers sometimes just to see them. I wish I could get far away enough from my own life to look at it like a stranger, see my own life from a distance and see it as all right. My mother is chewing and looking at me.

"What are you going to do?" she says. I shrug.

"I think I'm gonna sleep for about three days."

Leaving

Mina stopped in Lorene's kitchen to write David a note. She wanted to say something about how leaving was such a cliché thing, and to apologize for that. But instead she just said she was off with Lorene for a little break. Lorene stood by the door in her amber-tinted sunglasses, cell phone in one hand and car keys in the other.

"Shake a leg, doll."

"I'm ready," Mina said, pasting a stamp on the envelope and leaving it in Lorene's mailbox.

In the ordinary moments of the past, in the uninterpreted, free-floating, sense-organized memories of childhood, she was inclined to look for clues. To rake over the randomness, to evaporate feelings and look for telltale facts. Why? Because she had convinced herself there was a moment in which these things were decided. What they were all too dense to notice. Where things could have been different. Or maybe he was this way all along. Now they know how to interpret him, put his oddness and dysfunction in perspective. The fragility was always in him. The family is absolved. OK, but if either scenario is true, how come Mina was just like him through all those years? How come they were so close they didn't even have to whisper to each other, they just knew? How come one day it was this way with Mina and Michael, and the next day it was not? One day the mirror was there, the next day splintered in a thousand pieces? Because that's how it seemed to her, that sudden—like a thing shattering. And she couldn't do anything to change it.

CODA

"She's not here, she left," Lisa says. Michael is in the doorway of Lorene's house. Michael nods. He smiles at Lisa for a minute. She has the door open just a crack. He isn't as shiny as Lisa imagined Lorene's friends might be. He looks slight and frail.

"Just like that, huh?" Michael says.

"Seemed like she was running away." Lisa looks at Michael's face. He smiles at her again, then looks down to where Alex and Alisa peer from behind her legs.

"What a funny thing, uh, uh . . ."

"Lisa."

"Lisa, to run away when you live by yourself."

"Yeah," Lisa says.

"Between you and me, Lisa, I think Lorene is, well, she's a little nuts." He laughs at this. "I'm Michael," he says.

She nods. He gets hunched down and holds out his hand to Alisa and Alex. She sees he's sweating and although he looks kind of shaky and pretty grubby, she starts to think maybe he needs to eat, or rest. That's the first thing that occurs to her. And before she can think about it too much, Alex pushes in front of her legs.

"Hey, do you wanna come to my birthday party?" he says to Michael. Lisa smiles, and Michael nods seriously.

"Well, when is your birthday?" Michael asks Alex.

"Today, I think, Mom," Alex says, looking at his mother and nodding.

"About three months from now," Lisa says. She watches Alex watch Michael, his small body leaning forward, his hands balled into fists of excitement. Of course they want to see other people. Faintly, somewhere behind that, she feels something else. About herself. The only adult she's spoken to in days is the woman at the supermarket.

"Do you mind if I get a glass of water?" Michael says the words, then Lisa nods. She stands there nodding and there is a pause and then she opens the door. Is it desperation or optimism that makes people take risks, or start to long for things?

"I'll get the water," Lisa says. "Have a seat." Michael sits on the couch. He is sweating and he smiles weakly at her. He holds his head for a second, then looks around Lorene's living room. Alex and Alisa are standing by the arm of the couch, staring at the man their mother has led into the living room. Lisa looks at them for a moment, then leaves them and goes into the kitchen. She gets the filtered water out of the refrigerator and fills a glass with ice. Ice also made from filtered water. Good, clean, pure water. The ice cracks when she fills the glass, and she decides to get some cookies out and put them on a small plate. This is something she is really good at, taking care of people, and she likes doing it. She feels most like herself doing it, she is aware of this, also.

Lisa pushes open the kitchen door with her shoulder, balancing the glass of water and the dish of cookies in each hand. Michael leans against the arm of the couch. His eyes are closed and he is breathing heavily. Lisa puts the glass and dish down.

"Hey, what's wrong with him?"

"He's sleeping, honey." Lisa sits on a chair across from the couch.

"Why?"

"He's tired, I guess. Now be quiet." Lisa reaches for a cookie, eating slowly as Michael sleeps. His hands have fallen away from his lap. Lisa notices he has many circle scars, maybe burns, on the tender skin on the underside of his upper arm. Over and over.

Lorene walks through New Orleans, she inhales the city. Its strangeness. The oldness and decay relieve her of things. She thinks about finding someone to talk to. Or not. She spends all day in a cafe reading a nineteenth-century novel she found in a secondhand store. How exhausted she feels, how she just wants to sit and do nothing. She watches the slightly worn-out city, the way it encourages her to do nothing, and she thinks she could stay awhile. "I think I'm falling in love," she says, in a postcard, which she plans to mail to Mina tomorrow. But when she gets up from the table, she leaves the card behind, already tired of the sentiment.

Mina wakes up on the couch at her mother's. She thinks she'll call David. Tell him she's coming back. Well, what else is there to do? She gets up and drinks coffee alone. She decides to take a walk through the park. It's early, but already the place is full of determined runners and people walking their dogs. She hasn't been in Central Park since she visited Michael at Columbia. Mina walks all the way to 116th Street, and over to the Columbia campus. It feels so long ago, another lifetime that she was here, the most desperate time in her life, worse even than right now. She had made herself forget how awful it felt, how lost she was. And it seems as she crosses the campus that she is able to remember it all for the first time, with nothing internal fixing it up. She actually has to walk here, on these streets.

A toothless man half-heartedly holds out a cup to her. She hands him a dollar.

She never fails to give money to vagrants and street people. Homeless people, bums, crazy people, damaged people. She stops no matter what and gives them something. She knows why she does this, why she gives them money: not out of sympathy for their suffering, not even out of pity, but as a talisman against them.

In the midst of the very worst year, the year her parents finally divorced, the year her fascination with not eating had quietly saturated every part of her existence, in the year of her deepest self-loathing, Mina called her brother at school. She had to escape. Although it was in the middle of midterm exams, he immediately insisted she get on the next plane to see him. He did this, insisted, at a time when surely he was barely holding it together. He'd already had one serious episode, perhaps even been hospitalized for a stint. She didn't know at the time. She was mostly thinking about her own troubles. She did not want him to see her because she was so ashamed of what she was, but he insisted, as he always did. When she arrived at his dorm in Johnson Hall, when she finally saw him, all her rules collapsed. He was there at the door, smiling and handsome. Somehow the strangers they had become to each other had retreated. He was old Michael again, or at least puttting on a good show of it. And it made her normal and OK, her old self, or at least a good show of it. They spent one great afternoon walking around the campus, not saying much, but feeling playful and happy. He took her to the large and unfinished cathedral only blocks from his dorm. "Cathedrals are nice places," he said, with no irony and no smirking. It had never occurred to him to go inside before. They felt hushed and humbled at the entrance. The light filtered through huge stained-glass panels. Mina was glad for the light and glad simply for those words, *stained glass*, words that seemed as mysterious and pleasing as the colored light itself, describing glass built to be shone through, designed to make something beautiful—sunlight—even more perfect, which seemed both full of hubris and nearly brilliant to her, not ethereal but human and touching. This was even more the case when she examined the figures portrayed in the stained glass—skiers and soccer players.

Mina sits on a bench by the cathedral.

So what if it ended there? Couldn't that be the way it went? But there was more, and Mina couldn't stop thinking of it now. The relentlessness of memory—she wanted to remember slowly and accurately, not mess the order, so she could find her way to thinking about it.

He left school later that semester, just missing his graduation. There was an incident of some kind—why didn't she know exactly? He tried to return the next year but went back into the hospital. To stay for a long time. He wanted to. Yes, that's it, that's what she was trying to remember. This part. He never asked her to visit. But he wouldn't have to, would he? Finally, after six weeks she did go. He looked so awful, gray-skinned and with those burns under his bathrobe. He was blank and silent. He smoked cigarettes and stared through her. The place was painted that green-yellow hospital color. The vague urine scent in the room, overlaid with peroxide and ammonia. And did she grab Michael and kiss him and hold his hand? Did she visit him again and try to bring him around? Did she tell him it would be all right? Did she ever even once write him back? It was unbearable for her to see him like this, this wasn't her brother. What the fuck are all these cigarette burns? Mina wanted to scream. Why do you suck your cigarette like that? But she said nothing. It was part of the distance she had with him, had to have. Because she really didn't want to know. After that one time, she never visited him in the hospital, no matter how often he asked. She was busy. She'd see him when he got out. It was better for him. She would just upset him. She was so busy. She simply refused to see him this way. And somehow, after enough time, the estrangement became ordinary and everyday. Eventually it became something she didn't think about, pushed back into a secret compartment of her life.

Her mother said it was all the same, anyway. Wouldn't have made a difference. But Mina knows better: it would have made a difference right now, remembering this. It would have made a difference right now if she had just done just the smallest bit better. It would make a difference to her.

Mina thinks, Lorene, I wish you were here. If you were here now, I would tell you there are people who with the tiniest kindnesses can save your life, and if we understood that, just the extraordinary effect of the measliest attempts to comfort each other, even just that, we might lead very different lives.

And Lorene would say, Natch. Of course, doll.

Lisa isn't sure exactly what has happened, she is trying to figure out how to think about it. It is certainly bad, though, isn't it? Alex and Alisa are crying, and she is trying to comfort them. They both fight her when she pulls them into her arms. They cry to each other, not to her. They are, in fact, crying at her.

Michael had finally woken up after half an hour or so of sleeping. Lisa had been in the room the whole time, watching him and keeping the kids occupied with a board game on the floor. Michael woke up with a start, sitting upright on the couch. He looked dizzy for a moment, eyes quickly scanning the room. He jumped up from the couch and looked frantically behind him, and then finally at the three of them on the floor. Lisa smiled at him, cautiously, but already she felt a sick surge of anxiety, a physical thing, a wave through her spine and in her shoulders. He didn't smile back, she remembers, but stared wildly at her, confused, wide-eyed.

"Where am I?" he said. Lisa stopped smiling, she felt parts of herself sinking, even falling. The strange sensation of adrenaline starting to edge in.

"Lorene's house." Still he stared at her, disoriented. He glanced from her to the room and back again.

"What?"

"The hills above Hollywood Boulevard. Lorene Baker's house."

He took a deep breath and nodded, closing his eyes.

"What's wrong with you?" she said, but the question had more fear than concern in its tone, didn't it? It sounded like an accusation. She was no longer on the floor, but standing. Alisa and Alex were watching her and watching Michael. There was perhaps a second, a tiny pause, in which the four of them took in one another.

"I'm so sorry, I didn't mean to spook you, did I spook you, I'm so sorry," Michael probably said. Something like that. And Lisa thinks she remembers this vaguely, but actually, she is almost certain that Michael started to cry.

"What is wrong with you?" she said again, and she heard herself sounding angry. Alisa grabbed her calf and started to cry.

"A lot. I'm so sorry," Michael said, and his nose was running a little and he wiped it with the back of his hand and sniffed. The scars again.

Lisa frowned. "You have to leave now."

Michael looked at her wearily and didn't move.

"Leave now," she said again. She put her hand on Alisa's head and stared at him. Michael got up finally and started to walk, then stopped.

"What?" she said.

"I'm so sorry."

Lisa double-bolted the door behind him and watched him until he left the steps at the bottom of the walkway. She watched him through pulled-shut curtains. And, yes, for a few seconds after, she watched. While they cried.

"You never can tell about people, now can you?" she says. The kids continue to cry. Sob, more like. She realizes she is shaking a bit. Odder still, the sinking feeling hasn't left. She almost thinks she might have got it all wrong. She is so tired. What has happened? She's prettty sure she's getting everything wrong. She is so exhausted. She watches her children, bewildered. No mistaking it. Alex and Alisa are crying at her.

Lorene sits in an expensive restaurant on the edge of the French Quarter. She looks at her hands, not really recognizing them. She puts them under the table, suddenly self-conscious. She thinks about calling Mina, seeing how it all went. Truth is, she is kind of dying to talk to Mina, misses her in a bored, sentimental way. She doesn't mind that, either. She eats her dinner slowly and studies the staff as they work. Lorene examines silverware and feels with two fingers the paper the menu is printed on. She lifts the bread plate, a lovely simple bone china, to see if she has correctly guessed the name of the manufacturer. Of course, and this pleases her. The waitress stands by her table as Lorene engages her in conversation. After a couple of minutes of talking, the waitress nods distractedly, looks away for a second. Oh, God, Lorene thinks, it's happening—I'm becoming one of those people who tries to have personal conversations with waiters.

Mina gets up, washes her face. She takes a shower. She dresses and eats breakfast. She gathers her things together and boards a plane for L.A. She would have dinner with David that night. Which seems, at this long-distanced point, pretty good. Something everyday and ordinary and deeply familiar.

Mina stretches in her seat on the airplane, half watches the inflight film with no headphones.

Last night Lorene had called her from New Orleans. Woke her up. Lorene said she would be going back to California in a few days. Mina said, "It's only been a week, Lorene."

But it seems Lorene has a great idea for a new restaurant. Something so diabolically clever that it requires an in-person meeting of Pleasure Model Enterprises. It had come to Lorene suddenly, eureka-ish, in a lightning voodoo moment sometime between her paraffin pedicure and her painful but necessary Brazilian bikini wax.